CRAIG MARTELLE
MICHAEL ANDERLE

NOMAD REDEEMED

A KUTHERIAN GAMBIT SERIES
TERRY HENRY WALTON CHRONICLES
BOOK 2

DEDICATION

We can't write without those who support us
On the home front, we thank you for being there for us

We wouldn't be able to do this for a living if it weren't for our readers
We thank you for reading our books

Nomad Redeemed
The Terry Henry Walton Chronicles
Team Includes

BETA / EDITOR BOOK
Acknowledgements in Back!

JIT Beta Readers - From both of us, our deepest gratitude!
Norman Meredeth
Sherry Foster

*If I missed anyone, **please** let me know!*

COPYRIGHT

END TIMES ALASKA SERIES,
A WINLOCK PRESS PUBLICATION

Book 1: Endure
Book 2: Run
Book 3: Return
Book 4: Fury

RICK BANIK THRILLERS

People Raged and the Sky Was on Fire
The Heart Raged (2017)

SHORT STORY CONTRIBUTIONS TO ANTHOLOGIES

Earth Prime Anthology, Volume 1
(Stephen Lee & James M. Ward)
Apocalyptic Space Short Story Collection
(Stephen Lee & James M. Ward)
Lunar Resorts Anthology, Volume 2
(Stephen Lee & James M. Ward)
Just One More Fight
(published as a novella standalone)
The Expanding Universe, Volume 1
(edited by Craig Martelle)
The Expanding Universe, Volume 2
(edited by Craig Martell – June 2017)
The Misadventures of Jacob Wild McKilljoy
(with Michael-Scott Earle)
Metamorphosis Alpha, Stories from the Starship
Warden
(with James M. Ward – Summer 2017)

KUTHERIAN GAMBIT SERIES TITLES INCLUDE:

FIRST ARC

Death Becomes Her (01) - Queen Bitch (02) - Love Lost (03) - Bite This (04) - Never Forsaken (05) - Under My Heel (06) - Kneel Or Die (07)

SECOND ARC

We Will Build (08) - It's Hell To Choose (09) - Release The Dogs of War (10) - Sued For Peace (11) - We Have Contact (12) - My Ride is a Bitch (13) - Don't Cross This Line (14)

THIRD ARC *(Due 2017)*

Never Submit (15) - Never Surrender (16) - Forever Defend (17) - Might Makes Right (18) - Ahead Full (19) - Capture Death (20) - Life Goes On (21)

New Series

THE SECOND DARK AGES

The Dark Messiah
The Darkest Night *(04.2017)*
Darkest Before the Dawn *(07.2017)*
Light Is Breaking *(11.2017)*

THE BORIS CHRONICLES
With Paul C. Middleton

Evacuation
Retaliation
Revelation (*Dec 2016*)
Restitution (*2017*)

RECLAIMING HONOR
With Justin Sloan

Justice Is Calling (01)
Claimed By Honor (02)

THE ETHERIC ACADEMY
With TS Paul

ALPHA CLASS (01) (*Dec 2016/Jan 2017*)
ALPHA CLASS (02) (*Feb/Mar 2017*)
ALPHA CLASS (03) (*May/June 2017*)

TERRY HENRY "TH" WALTON CHRONICLES
With Craig Martelle

See above!

SHORT STORIES

Frank Kurns Stories of the Unknownworld 01 (*7.5*)
You Don't Mess with John's Cousin

Frank Kurns Stories of the Unknownworld 02 (*9.5*)
Bitch's Night Out

Frank Kurns Stories of the Unknownworld 03 (13.25)
BELLATRIX
With Natalie Grey

ANTHOLOGIES

Glimpse
Honor in Death
(Michael's First Few Days)

Beyond the Stars: At Galaxy's Edge
Tabitha's Vacation

CRAIG MARTELLE SOCIAL

For a chance to see ALL of Craig's new Book Series
Check out his website below!

Website:
http://www.craigmartelle.com

Email List:
http://www.craigmartelle.com
(Go 1/2 way down his first page, the box is in the center!)

Facebook Here:
https://www.facebook.com/AuthorCraigMartelle/

MICHAEL ANDERLE SOCIAL

Website:
http://kurtherianbooks.com/

Email List:
http://kurtherianbooks.com/email-list/

Facebook Here:
https://www.facebook.com/TheKurtherianGambitBooks/

PROLOGUE

That wasn't good enough for TH. He wanted to search for the stockpile. He hunted Mark down to let him know. "You take this group back to New Boulder. Char and I are going to search for the stockpile," Terry informed him.

Mark was instantly boiling mad. "That's bullshit!" he yelled. "You sell these people on a better world, and then you bail on them? You're not going anywhere except back north with us. Do you understand me?" Mark crossed his arms and stood with feet spread wide.

"That's not how it works. I give the orders, and you follow them," Terry said coldly.

"Is your white whale out there somewhere, Terry Henry Walton? I'm begging you, come with us." Mark's eyes were wide as he unfolded his arms and clasped his hands in front of him, pleading with Terry to change his mind. "Search for your mystical Nirvana later."

"Can't you take them on your own?" Terry asked.

There was a pause before Mark admitted, "Of course I can, but it's not about that. It's about *you* being the leader we need you to be, the person who's going to bring civilization back to us. I can take them to New Boulder, but I can't do the rest of it." Mark pointed to Terry, "That's you, bastard," he said, gaining confidence in being an upstart.

"Fuck me …" Terry hung his head and looked at the ground. Char slapped him on the back while Clyde nuzzled his leg. The people watched, wondering what he was going to do.

CHAPTER ONE

The mountain lion wanted the deer as much as Sawyer Brown's people did. Two men tried to push him away, but he snarled and slashed at their meager walking sticks. He grabbed the carcass and started to drag it backwards away from the offending humans. The people watched, helplessly. One man, Devlin was running from the front of the long, drawn out line of people and another two from the back. The two from the back were closing at an unnatural speed.

Terry Henry Walton and Charumati ran straight for the deer, wondering where Mark had disappeared to after shooting the animal, leaving the poor people from Brownsville to fend for themselves.

Terry stopped at fifty yards away and dropped to a knee. As he aimed his M4 combat rifle, Char continued to run past, heading straight for the mountain lion. She veered out of his line of sight for an instant, all he needed to pull the trigger. The round hit the great creature between the eyes as it released the deer and prepared to fight the werewolf. Char leapt and landed on the thing as it dropped dead.

She growled her dismay at not getting to fight her fellow predator, but, realizing the risk she had taken, quickly relaxed. As far as she knew, her secret of being a Werewolf was safe. She didn't know that Terry risked hitting her to help her keep that secret.

She stood up and brushed herself off, suggesting they skin the mountain lion and keep the hide. There was always something to be done with such a magnificent pelt.

Terry walked up beside her, "So, you decided that fighting a mountain lion barehanded was your best course of action? Is there any reason to carry pistols if you're not going to use them?" He asked sarcastically. Sometimes he wondered how hard she was trying to keep her secret.

"Oh, those? I didn't need those to fight that little thing," she replied innocently as she pointed to the cat. The others started cleaning the deer, and one man looked proud that he was the one given the opportunity to skin a mountain lion.

When Devlin arrived, out of breath from his run, he was happy that no one got hurt, but miffed at having run all that way for no reason.

Terry looked around, his eyes narrowed. "Where in the hell did Mark go? He should have been here," he spat out, not at Devlin, but he was angry.

"Squirts," Devlin answered, keeping his voice low and shrugging. He knew Terry wasn't mad at him. He turned and then jogged slowly back toward the front of the line leaving the two of them behind.

"Break!" Terry yelled in his Marine voice, projecting well

past the running man. The people stopped walking and found places to sit. Devlin looked back, shaking his head as Terry smiled.

Mark finally appeared, looking miserable. There was nothing anyone could do for him. He must have eaten something undercooked or gotten water that was bad. It would pass with enough good water and better food, like the venison they were cutting up.

Terry Henry remained gloomy as they walked north, toward New Boulder. Char stayed by his side and laughed the entire time because he didn't get his way. Clyde seemed indifferent to it all and was more than happy to feast on mountain lion when the time came. Terry thought it would be inedible, but this was the Wasteland and food was hard to come by.

He asked the man skinning the great cat to butcher it as well. The man did as he was told, keenly stripping the meat and piling it onto the inside of the hide.

Terry told a pair of young men to build a fire to cook their kill. There wasn't any firewood handy so they conscripted more of the people from Brownsville to search for anything that would burn.

As the refugees returned with bits and pieces of Wasteland scrub, Terry helped the men build a field smoker. He stole a blanket from the travois, hoping it wasn't someone's bedroll. It would help contain the smoke and that would preserve the meat long enough that they didn't have to eat it in one sitting, although they were getting low on food. A total of thirty-six people and twelve horses were headed north on a trip over 100 miles, most of which was through the Wastelands east of Denver.

The Wastelands weren't as bad as they used to be, some people thought. Terry had lived out there, he knew all about it.

For a while anyway, if you call what he did living.

And he agreed. The climate was changing, getting a little cooler with each year. Terry preferred to think of it as less brutal as opposed to cooler.

Terry stood and walked the line of people, stroking the grazing horses' necks as he passed. The people waved and greeted him kindly. He shook hands and refused to look at them like the refugees they might feel like they were. Rather, he'd told them that there was work, a new and better life that they could make for themselves.

He hoped Billy Spires saw things that way. Terry decided to ride ahead and make his own luck by preparing Billy and New Boulder for the influx of refugees.

◈ ◈ ◈

There was a sudden bang from a kick to the wall. "It's been three weeks. Those fuckers bailed on us! Son of a bitch. I just started to trust that bastard, too." Billy delivered his latest tirade while looking out the window, as he had been doing much too often.

Felicity drawled, trying to calm Billy down. "Billy, let's go to the power plant, see how things are progressing, and then we can go to the greenhouses. We didn't go yesterday and all that does is drive you deeper into that black pit of yours. Let it go. We will find out in due time. We've had no surprises over the past three weeks, have we? Isn't that something? Think what you want, but I believe that Mr. Terry Henry Walton has been successful in driving the bad men away. They would have returned by now if they could. Pretty soon the weather won't allow it, will it, Billy dear?"

Billy faced her, frowning, shoulders sagging. "I know

you're right, but I just can't get past the feeling that I've been double-crossed."

"Billy. Seriously. What has Terry Henry done that would suggest he wouldn't come back? Mark and those others. You think Ivan would run away? I don't know about Char, but it doesn't add up that they'd leave us high and dry. They didn't take anything of yours. The horses, their rifles, they took those from the others. Sure, Terry has your rifle and pistol, but there wasn't much ammunition for them, was there?" Felicity argued, saving her best for last. "Don't forget about his beer!"

She pointed in the direction where it had been fermenting. "If nothing else, he's a man and that is the only beer that's been available for the past twenty years. He'll be back, not for you or me," she pointed to him then herself, "but for his *beer*."

He slowly started to nod, then shrugged his shoulders. Billy didn't understand why he found that argument compelling, but he did and it put his mind at ease.

Felicity had gone to see Margie Rose and asked that she make Billy a new shirt at the very least. He'd worn that one for six weeks before Felicity threatened to burn it and leave him with nothing.

Billy wore the patchwork shirt that Margie Rose had put together for him, and Felicity had a hard time not shaking her head. She'd created this situation through her hasty actions. She was the one who had to look at it. Even twenty years after, she believed that people could still show a little class, like what she'd done for Char, getting her new clothes, a hairstyle, and makeup after the last battle.

Putting her envy of the tall beauty aside, Felicity determined that killing her with kindness would have to do. That woman was far too dangerous for a cat fight.

Billy watched Felicity's mind work. He wondered what she was thinking about, but shrugged it off and decided that they'd head out, do as she recommended.

They walked downstairs together and out the front door, where the sound of horses trotting on pavement greeted them.

The two looked towards the new arrivals. "What did I tell you?" Felicity beamed.

❖ ❖ ❖

Terry, Char, and Clyde left the caravan of travelers behind, riding ahead to find a place for the people to stay and set them up for as quick an integration as possible into what passed for a society in New Boulder. For that, they needed Billy Spires.

They were surprised to see him and Felicity standing outside, as if they had been expected.

"Billy! I think we have some news that you'd like to hear," Terry said as he and Char climbed off their horses. Clyde greeted his new humans, getting petted by each, before racing off after a rabbit, braying as he trailed the small creature. The four had turned to watch him go.

Billy crossed his arms, saying nothing as he glared at his security chief. Felicity punched him in the back and brushed past to give Terry a hug, that probably lasted too long, before she moved on to hug Char as well.

Billy shook his head and put out his hand.

Terry took it and grinned, giving the mayor an update. "No one hurt on our side, and we have thirty-one people inbound, ready to join us here in New Boulder, and they are ready to work." Terry stated, pointing to the belt and pistols around Char's waist. "Sawyer Brown didn't survive our negotiations, unfortunately. We have twelve horses, rifles, and ammunition.

We didn't find the stash I was looking for, but for our first expedition, I'm not sure we could have done better."

When Billy let the silence continue for too long, Char asked, "They'll be here soon. Where can we house them until they can get their own places, integrate into the community?" He looked at her oddly, almost as if he didn't understand.

His eyes opened wide in recognition, "Well I'll be God-damned! This whole fucking time I've been thinking you weren't coming back and then here you are. What the hell? We've got work to do!" He looked up and down the street, "Fuck! I've wasted three weeks. We need to get the people together, see who can open their homes, which homes are habitable, who needs help, make sure we put people where they know what they're doing. Are there any engineers, mechanics, maybe a doctor in that group?" Billy asked, after finally putting his mayor hat on as he recognized the avalanche of responsibilities that were walking right down the road into his town.

Billy punched Terry in the chest. "I'll be damned. I'm sorry I didn't trust you, Terry Henry Walton. Let's get these people settled and then let's talk about what's next. Son of a bitch! This is going to be a real town again." Billy was suddenly all smiles as he quivered with excitement.

Maybe getting old wasn't so bad. Changing his ways from the town bully to the town leader had happened almost without him noticing. Between Felicity and Terry, he knew he had no choice. Sometimes it was easier to go with the flow.

Char leaned conspiratorially toward Felicity. "Lots of nice looking young men in this bunch…" she whispered, slowly licking her lips before laughing at the look on Billy's face.

❖ ❖ ❖

Marcus leaned back, having just gorged on yet another elk. "Have you ever heard of a Werewolf getting fat?" he asked the half-asleep Ted sitting next to him.

Most conversations with Marcus were dangerous. Since before Charumati left, he'd been brooding, but things had only gotten worse. Answers to seemingly innocuous questions were sometimes met with extreme violence. Ted tried to parse his words carefully.

"I have not, unless I was supposed to, then I did, but I can't remember," Ted replied.

"What? Why do I waste time asking an idiot like you anything? The answer is no, until now. I think I'm getting fat, but not so much that I can't kick your ass upside-down and backwards!" Marcus removed his clothes and changed into his werewolf form, a great beast, all black, with yellow eyes glaring at the physical world. He threw his head back and howled, summoning the others to him as his call shook the trees.

Ted scrambled away, changing form as soon as he managed to tear off his shirt and pants. The others howled from their perches around the small valley, then the sounds died away as they ran to join their alpha. Marcus found a rock from which he could look down on the valley, down on the others in the pack.

As they arrived, they howled to their alpha, then sat haphazardly around the area. The males--Ted, Simmons, Adams, and Merrit. The three remaining females--Sue, Xandrie, and Shonna. Two of the females were coming into heat. Marcus wondered which of the others he'd have to fight for them, but he was ready. He kept his pack only strong enough that no one could challenge him. His mate wasn't there to constrain any challenge he might like to make, as it was an alpha's right. Many Alpha's didn't exercise that right, letting the she-wolves choose their mates, but Marcus had been alone for long enough that he didn't care about the old ways.

He cared about his way.

"It's time we return to the foothills, get Char, and go south," he told them, not inviting discussion. They watched silently, eyes gleaming in the darkness. He missed the purple eyes of his contentious mate, eyes changed by a chance injection of nanocytes into her body before the fall. She healed more quickly than any other Werewolf he knew about, but she had more human tendencies, too.

I shouldn't have let her go, Marcus thought, but she had left regardless, and that made him angry again. She was in his pack, and she needed to do as he ordered. He wanted her back so he could put her in her place once and for all.

Timmons howled to support his alpha. He had no choice. It was how the game was played.

CHAPTER TWO

Char sniffed the air outside the greenhouse. Crisp and clean. Fall was coming. There was a group of five newcomers with them since Billy decided everyone had to work the greenhouses and the fields before they determined where best to put people. Terry committed to learning about the newcomers to ensure the best fit between people and their work. Billy hadn't considered that a problem right away.

Terry didn't want the inevitable strife from people doing jobs they hated. Char was indifferent to it all, suggesting they should be happy they had food to eat and a warm place to sleep.

As odd as it sounded, just having food, water, and a warm bed would get old quickly as the lower levels on Maslow's hierarchy of needs were guaranteed. It was human nature to want more and better. Terry understood it because he was well read, and had intently studied why conflict started, and what could be done to prevent them.

And then there was beer. He saw that as the top rung on the ladder to enlightenment. This was the first time he'd been able to visit Pepe and Maria since he returned from their foray south. He rubbed his hands together and smiled.

"Look at you," Char said with her hands on her hips and chin up. "All you can think about is your damn beer, isn't it? It's like watching a little kid at Christmas."

He smacked his lips. "No matter how hard you try, you won't harsh my buzz!" Terry replied, grinning broadly.

Her mouth opened slightly. "Harsh your buzz? What are you, twelve? Don't answer that. I think you're trying to recapture the magic of your first beer, and that is when you stopped maturing. It's like Mecca for you," she added.

Terry grabbed her without hesitation, picking her up and swinging her around in a circle. She dug her robust fingernails into his neck to let him know that she had enough of his horseplay and ridiculous good mood.

James stood by placidly, watching. He had yet to figure out the relationship between those two. He thought they were married, but then heard they weren't. They acted like they'd been together forever. When James found out that she arrived a week after Terry, less than two months previously, he was confused.

He had a glimpse of her naked body when she distracted the men of Sawyer Brown's ambush. He thought they were doing it, but they hadn't been. He wondered how Terry could deny himself such a woman. Maybe one day James would find out, but then he suspected he didn't want to know the answer.

He dropped her down. "I promised you a beer, James,

and through those doors lies the promised land." Terry waved the group forward as he strode boldly into the greenhouse, where Pepe and Maria greeted them all, stopping the group. Terry looked past the two, but Pepe held out a hand to keep Terry from racing into the back.

"Welcome to our greenhouse..." Maria said, followed by a long list of platitudes as they were happy to have the help. She and Pepe wanted to set the expectations for the group regarding what work needed to be done, how to do it, and what they would get to take with them when they left.

Soon, Pepe and Maria would harvest the wheat, and they would need the help of every person they could find. But the amount of grain would be sufficient to bake bread through the winter.

Pepe and Maria also needed to plant the winter wheat field to give them a harvest in the summer. So much work, but with the new people, next year's harvest would be the biggest ever. Pepe beamed with joy.

Terry was feeling a lot less love and happiness being held back from his beer.

Terry made a small speech to the group, then turned them over to Maria as she handed out fresh baked rolls with her special cucumber dip. Terry physically pulled Pepe aside. He looked at the shorter man. "Why are you keeping me from my beer?" he growled. "What's wrong?"

Pepe smiled sheepishly. "It was ready a week ago, based on how you described it. I didn't want it to go bad, so I bottled it. I didn't know how to tell you, and I don't want you to be mad!" Pepe pleaded.

The surprise must have shown on Terry's face as Pepe winced. Char magically appeared wearing a concerned expression and holding her hands up as if ready to fight.

"You know what this means?" Terry asked. No one moved.

"That means the beer is ready now!" He grabbed Pepe by the shoulders and shook him joyously, then turned to Char. "Get me a beer, woman!" Char's fist shot out at the speed of thought, crunching into Terry's cheek, sending him staggering.

To his credit, he didn't fall. Pepe watched, wide-eyed.

"Holy fuck, Char! What the hell?" Terry grumbled, working his jaw to make sure nothing was broken. He checked his teeth with his tongue, searching for anything loose.

Char smiled pleasantly, then wrapped an arm in Pepe's. "Show me this magical elixir known as beer, so I can see why it turns grown men into little boys."

James was more confused than ever. "Are they married?" he asked. Maria shrugged. The rest watched the antics and ate in silence.

❖ ❖ ❖

Billy Spires had to run wherever he went because he had more to do than time in which to do it. Felicity had no interest in running and reminded Billy that he promised her a ride. He couldn't deliver, but he had an idea where to start.

He left Felicity at the greenhouse working with a group of new people as he ran back past his house and to the power plant. With the arrival of the cooler weather, Billy didn't even break a sweat as he journeyed from one place to the next.

As he passed the streetlights, he admired them, knowing that they would be lit come nightfall. The power was already surging through the lines, one house at a time getting added to the burgeoning electrical grid. Some of the newcomers were given homes that would soon have power. All the people had to do was repair the house, fix some things, and do it in their spare time after splitting a full day's work between the fields and cutting firewood.

None of the newcomers complained. They were able to eat and no one was beaten. Terry and the FDG weren't too keen on people using violence to get what they wanted. Some of the new men quickly learned that Sawyer's way of getting what he wanted was the wrong way. Anyone trying to emulate it received a harsh lesson in new world peacekeeping.

Although Terry believed that it took violence to stop violence, he also believed that a pat on the back and a friendly helping hand needed to be given first and often. Only after that did he dispense justice, and Terry gave those beat-downs all by himself. He didn't want any of the others to think they were better than the newcomers. Terry hated doing it, but preferred that over the Force getting a reputation as goons.

He couldn't have that.

So Terry Henry Walton, security chief for New Boulder, kept the peace, while also seeking to grow the Force de Guerre. He wanted new recruits to double the size of his unit, and then he'd keep doubling it until he had an entire army.

Because that was what it would take to tame the Wastelands. Billy Spires considered himself a benevolent dictator, and the more Terry thought about it, the land required a strongman, not a democracy. You could only have that level of freedom once your security was guaranteed. Terry didn't want to be the benevolent dictator, but he embraced his role as the honest broker. He'd let the dictator be benevolent, but if Billy went too far, Terry would pull him back in.

TH's mission was to bring civilization back to humanity. He'd do what he had to until the people had a say in their future and free elections supported them in that.

◈ ◈ ◈

Terry looked at Char as she dug through refuse they found in one of the homes destined for the newcomers. Doubling and tripling up was useful only until they had space and supplies for people to have their own homes. They were trying to build a civilization, not a place where they stacked people up like cordwood.

Members of the FDG were conducting surveys, marking a map as they went.

"Would you look at this!" Char exclaimed, removing clothing from a sealed plastic bag. She shook it out and held the jacket up to herself. It was a military uniform that someone had probably sealed as a keepsake. It was much too large for her. She handed it over, and Terry held it up.

"With a little of Margie Rose's fancy needlework, I think I might have something more fitting my station, don't you think?" Terry looked at the silver oak leaf insignia of a lieutenant colonel. He was good with that, even though it didn't really matter.

No one in this new world cared about that rank. They only knew that Terry Henry brought them peace of mind. Not silver leaves on a collar. Maybe someday people would equate those with a person of integrity. Not today, though.

Until then, Terry was the pillar of virtue, the Marine's Marine. The bringer of light.

When he looked up, Char was naked and trying to wriggle into a pair of jeans. She jumped up and down a couple times to get them over her hips. She shouted in joy as she fastened them, turning left and right to admire them. They were skin tight, but a little loose around the waist.

"What do you think?" she asked. Terry didn't answer,

wondering why her shirt was off while trying on jeans. That question was answered when she pulled a fluorescent orange bikini top out of the same bag. She adjusted the straps in the back and tried it on, took it off and made a couple other adjustments until it mostly fit. "And now?"

"I think you still need to wear your shirt," Terry said flatly. She smirked and put her flannel shirt back on, but didn't button it, only tied the lower ends around her waist. Terry knew that she wasn't affected by the cold like humans, but didn't want her to flaunt it.

Then again, she didn't know that he knew.

"Structurally sound? It could use a new roof, just like every home nowadays, but people could live here. It has a fireplace and an area to dig an outhouse. What else do they need?" Terry said to himself as he returned his focus to the survey. When he looked up, he found himself alone. He heard Char rummaging in a closet down the hallway.

Terry wondered why this home had not been pillaged over the years. He left Char to her search and went outside. Painted on the front and back doors was the bio-hazard symbol, almost faded to nothing. Would anything survive after twenty years?

He hoped not, but would encourage a full scrubbing with some of the homemade vinegar that seemed prevalent in New Boulder. Vinegar was every bit as hard to make as beer, maybe more so until the base cultures were sound. After that, the batch sizes could grow. It was a foul-smelling process, but the end result was worth the effort, giving them anything from a cleaning solution to salad dressing.

A skeleton sprawled on the back porch. Terry thought that was a nice touch to keep the weaker people away, especially in the first year after the World's Worst Day Ever. He kicked it into a bush, then checked the house for any structural shortcomings, like a cracked foundation or a bowed load-bearing wall. He didn't find anything that suggested the house would fall on its inhabitants.

When he returned inside, Char was barely able to peer above an armload of material and yarn. "Let's get this back to Margie Rose. We have some work to do!" she exclaimed. Terry looked at the fatigues he'd been absentmindedly carrying.

"Sounds good. Let's ditch this stuff and get back out here, finish our survey. The people need to know where they can live before winter hits us in the face," Terry answered.

"Don't we have enough places scoped out? There probably isn't enough firewood to go around as it is. Maybe we shouldn't give them so many choices?" She raised her eyebrows to emphasize her point since she couldn't use her hands. Her purple eyes seemed to glow in the faint indoor light.

"Because it's just what we need to do. We'll probably take the FDG out with the first snowfall. It'll be easier to see where other survivors are holed up. I want to make sure that we've settled things here, that's all."

Char didn't seem convinced. He didn't know werewolves had clothing fetishes. He wondered if she had been equally addicted to shoe shopping when there was such a thing.

"Where are you from, Char? I mean really from, like where did you grow up, before the fall, that is?" he asked, more pointedly than he'd ever asked before.

"I'm not that old!" she attempted to dodge.

"You're like me, good genes. You had a life in the before time. You were somebody and now you're somebody again. I'm sure a little different than before, just like we all are," he countered.

"Fine, how about this?" she said, slipping into a hard New York accent. "Can you guess where I'm from now, Terry Henry Walton?"

"The city. When's the last time you were there? Is it still standing? Do you know anything about Chicago?" TH pried with rapid-fire questions, wanting more information. He hadn't left the western plains, and wanted to know.

"The city survived the fall of mankind, but not well. Too many people in too small a space. They ran out of food quickly and resorted to cannibalism. A few us went north, into Canada, and then worked our way west. Over the years we tried settling, but we'd always run out of food and then had to move on. When we hit the Rockies, we found the hunting was good and then moved south with the herds. That's when I went out on my own. I hunted until I found you, TH. It was like I was magically drawn to you." She blinked her eyes at him.

"You found Billy Spires, if I remember correctly," Terry replied coolly, wondering what her angle was this time.

"He was just the first person I ran across, but I was coming for you," she purred.

"Of course you were. I tell you what, why don't you take your haul back to Margie Rose, and here, take these, too," Terry said as he tossed the fatigues on top of her pile.

"See if Margie Rose can fit me into those. I'm going to the barracks and check on the boys. They might be back from work by now and we need to train and then do some recruiting. I want to double the size of the Force," Terry stated firmly.

"Okay," she replied happily and headed toward the front door. He opened it for her, and they walked down the steps together. She started running, and he watched her go.

"So that's what you wanted, which is what you said in

the first place…" Terry started talking to himself, then looked around quickly to make sure there was no one to notice his muttering, before continuing. "Fucking Werewolf, making me weird."

CHAPTER THREE

James was elbow deep in the dirt, working the soil within the greenhouse for the next planting. The harvest had gone well, but they were cleaning up for the rotational crop that was heartier for the cool of the winter, like kale, kohlrabi, and Brussels sprouts. James wanted to prove himself to Terry Henry because of all the people in his life, that man had treated him the most fairly.

Terry treated everyone the same way. James didn't know how to ask to join the Force, but that was what he wanted. He saw the other members, Mark and Devlin, work in the greenhouse, too. Everyone shared in the sacrifice to bring food to all, but then Terry would collect his men and they'd head out to train.

Train to be a real soldier! James thought, smiling inwardly. Sawyer Brown was just a bully, but he knew how to fight. Terry knew how to fight, too, better than Sawyer could have ever been. And Terry knew how to lead people. James decided that he'd follow that man anywhere.

James had skills, too. He was a new age mechanic, trained by his father as they tried to make a go of it themselves after the fall. Ten years they lasted, but then sickness took the rest of James's family. He wandered until he ran into Sawyer Brown, and after that, he just did as he was told.

James was good with his hands and had a basic understanding of how things worked. He would love a shot at the power plant, working with a real mechanic, but he hadn't told anyone because he didn't want to get stuck there. He wanted to be a soldier under Terry's command.

James watched the other people working the dirt. They looked happy. As was the case, each time the helpers showed up, the farmers fed them a light meal and after getting general guidance on the day's tasks, the workers were turned loose. They worked hard with little conversation, happy to be indoors and happy to be well fed.

Not everyone was happy, though.

James watched the farmer get more and more frustrated while working on the water pump. James finished his row, then hustled over to the man.

Stepping close, he said, "I have some experience working with these. Maybe I can help?" he offered. The farmer thrust an old wrench at James, throwing his hands up in disgust and storming away. James watched him go, "I'll take that as a yes?" he shrugged his shoulders as the farmer disappeared into bushes toward the back of the greenhouse.

James looked at the rudimentary hand pump. It wouldn't hold prime. James figured a gasket had gone bad or some bushings had failed. He tore it down, seeing how it had been roughly fixed over the years and amazed that it had worked at all. He cleaned off the previous repairs, determined that he needed to do some ad hoc welding to build up the metal and help create a new seal.

"Do you know where there's any copper?" he asked, but the farmer's wife didn't hear him. James explored outside the greenhouse and found the shed that all farmers had--a shed filled with a pile of junk. Some would call it inventory, defending their inability to throw anything away.

James found a few pieces of heavy copper wire and a heavily rusted cast iron pan. He found metal BBs that he could use as bearings if he had to.

He deposited his supplies at the fire pit behind the greenhouse. He returned to the pump, picking up the pieces carefully and cradling them as he took them to the fire pit. He started a small fire, then built it up while making a rough bellows out of worn tarp and two-by-fours. He angled the cast iron into the fire, with the copper sitting inside. With his bellows, he drove the fire hotter and hotter. When the copper melted and rolled around inside the cast iron, James cheered for a minute, a smile lit up his face before it slowly receded and he scratched his chin after a moment.

James realized he wasn't sure how to deposit the copper one drip at a time on the worn internal structure of the pump. First, he tried a stick, but that added too much dirt. Then, he rolled his shirt so he could grip the pan's handle and tried a careful effort to drip it out of the pan, but he dripped too much copper at one location. James used the wrench to get some of the copper into place, but it wouldn't stick.

He put the pump case into the pan and put the whole thing in the fire. After two more logs and more furious bellows pumping, he found the copper stuck enough to build up the fitting, a little at a time, until both cooled too much to work with.

James hoped it was enough. He had burns up and down his arms and across his bare chest where the copper had splattered.

The tattoos of a blacksmith, he smirked.

He ladled water onto the outside structure. He only wanted it cool enough to put the key pieces back together. The copper could pull free from the steel if he cooled both metals too quickly.

He jammed it back together and turned the crank slowly in the hopes that the motion would help shape the moving parts against the fixed structure. He gave it fifteen more minutes before the metal was cool enough to touch.

Then he waited fifteen more before he reinstalled the pump. As he was doing that, the Farmer came back and watched, quietly. James added a little pig fat that the farmer had been using as grease. When James finally turned the handle, he could hear the air being pushed through as the pump sought to prime itself and pull water from underground.

When the water started to flow, the farmer howled in joy. The water volume was far greater than anything the man could remember. He clapped James on the back hard enough to drive the young man to his knees. The farmer took over and happily pumped away, filling the irrigation troughs with little effort. "You're hired!" he bellowed as he called everyone over to look at the pump.

James was slightly embarrassed, not used to being the center of attention, but proud to have made the farmer's day.

He looked around at all of the onlookers. If only Terry Henry was there to see.

❖ ❖ ❖

After Terry rousted the boys for some impromptu calisthenics and a short, five-mile run, he turned them loose for weapons cleaning and maintenance, followed by horse grooming and stable cleaning. None of the men were happy about an endless list of chores, but none of them complained.

He called them together for one last word.

"Gentlemen, we need to be ready. When the first snow falls, we're taking the show on the road." They looked at him oddly. Even Mark hadn't heard the expression before. "We're going out to look for other survivors. They'll be easier to find with the snow and the cold. That means you need to dig out your winter clothes and a good coat."

"Sir?" Mark asked. With a nod, he continued. "You've been out there. What do we expect to find?"

Terry thought about it a moment before answering Mark's question. "Stragglers, families, maybe even a small community. We want them to come here, and we'll offer that option, but it'll be up to them to accept. We'll give them food, the option to join us, and then we'll leave them to it. I think more will come than not, but that's just my guess."

"The Force could use more people, a presence out in the Wasteland and one here," Mark said, hands up as he held a defensive posture.

"I've been thinking that same thing, Mark. We need to recruit some of Sawyer's boys. I tell you what, let's set up a little recruiting center for them and see what we get. We'll spread the word tomorrow and then interview the volunteers the day after. Sound good, gentlemen?" Terry asked.

They agreed, slapping each other on the back.

"Don't be afraid to share your ideas or ask a question.

Think how smart we'll be if we all use our minds at the same time," Terry told them.

He turned the Force over to Mark to complete the day's tasks.

Mark nodded, gave a rough salute, and turned to the men he had--Jim, Devlin, and Ivan.

Terry left at a jog, deciding not to take a horse. The grazing behind Margie Rose's house was bad, and he thought the horses deserved better.

Terry made quick work of the run, Clyde keeping up as he always did. They slowed to a walk a quarter-mile before the house so he could cool down. When he arrived, he found Char modeling a shirt that Margie Rose had sewn for her with a swath of the new material.

There was nothing on the stove and after his little run and cool down, he was hungry. Terry's turn to cook was yesterday. Clyde was equally confused, so much so that the dog checked the stove and the counter before finding a place on the couch.

Char danced up to Terry and gave him a kiss on the cheek. "What do you think, TH?" She spun around for him to see the new outfit that Margie Rose had sewn from the material they'd found earlier in the day.

"What does it matter what I think?" Terry asked, coming across as an ass. Margie Rose was on him in an instant, waving her ever-present wooden spoon.

"You apologize right now, mister! Can't you see two inches in front of your face? Can't you see that this woman is head over heels in love with you, and then you say something like that! You'll be sleeping outside, mister, if you don't pull your head out of that place where the sun doesn't shine!" That was as bold as Margie Rose would get in creative cursing.

"But she's a…" Terry stopped himself from saying *Were-wolf*, but that was what he was thinking. Why did a Werewolf care what the lowly Terry Henry Walton thought? Discretion was the better part of valor. This was not the right time for this battle. "I am so sorry, Char! You look magnificent. Let's see the rest of you."

Char looked skeptical at Terry's sudden change of heart, but Margie Rose was sufficiently pleased to tuck her spoon back into its apron pocket.

"You look fine. It's hard to complain about how those jeans look on you," he added, eyeing Margie Rose carefully. She beamed, before turning and going into the kitchen.

"Ah, dinner," he whispered to himself, but Char heard it clearly.

"I thought that was it. Maybe you're thinking that your bitch can go get you a beer?" she asked, although it wasn't a question.

Terry's ears perked up, but he wouldn't fall for it for two reasons. Firstly, he would never ask her to get him a beer again. The nanocytes took two days to repair the damage from the last time, and secondly, although she was a she-wolf, literally a bitch, he would never call her that.

"Absolutely not!" he answered. "But I will get you one if you like?"

"*What*? That is the most foul concoction I have ever smelled. I can't imagine putting any of what is in those bottles in my mouth." Her face contorted with the thought of the smell, which, not surprisingly, made him want one even worse.

He excused himself to go outside and pull one of his precious jars from the shaded crawl space of the house. It was cool enough outside that it was almost like drinking a cold beer, except for the fact that it was still too warm and Char was right. It was really foul-tasting.

But there had been no other beer for a lifetime. He wondered if he was mis-remembering the taste. He took another sip.

Nope. It was bad.

He put the jar up to his nose and inhaled deeply. The mash was too heavy. Cut the recipe in half or double the water, maybe prime it with a touch of cherry juice or something before bottling.

Terry was a fan of man-law that declared no fruit in beer, but twenty years after the fall of civilization, maybe the law was outdated. He brought his beer inside, sipping it slowly, trying not to gag, while making a show of smacking his lips and saying, "Ahhh."

Clyde wouldn't even drink the beer, and Terry had seen his dog eat a rat that had been dead for a week.

CHAPTER FOUR

Marcus sat on the same bluff where he'd last seen his mate. He could sense her in the town far below. He knew there were humans, too, more than before. He wanted to know what that was about. He expected he'd have to walk into the town and find out for himself, find her, and bring her home.

He crouched on a rock and watched while the rest of the pack spread out nearby, silent as they wondered about their next move.

Marcus continued to be angry about everything. The bitches hadn't gone into heat, and he hated being wrong about things like that. He'd been posturing and baiting their mates, and despite some nibbles, he didn't get the combat he craved with the spoils as were his due.

As the alpha, the others would submit, and that wasn't combat. He wanted a real fight, and he suspected what he wanted was down there.

He watched as three hunters rode horses into the foothills and then turned north. Men with rifles. Men who would fight. The date with his mate would have to wait. He looked at the others, then changed into his werewolf form. They followed and soon, the pack was running freely through the woods, looking for a place where they could wait for the hunters.

❖ ❖ ❖

James was staying in a house with three other men and one couple. Most of them were older. They seemed to have little ambition, but that was probably from the upheaval in their lives ever since they met Sawyer Brown. That man had darkened everyone's hopes, but had allowed them to continue their existence. Now they had hope, although they hadn't embraced it.

James had and felt like a new man. He was happy when he went to sleep, and still smiling when he woke up, having not been woken during the night by a madman, drunk with his own power.

The young man would keep working on them. There was nothing like being happy to improve the spirits of those around you.

With a quick breakfast of vegetables and venison sausage, the group headed for the greenhouses. On the way, they found four members from the Force waiting in the roadway. Mark, Devlin, Jim, and Ivan were armed with the AK-47s that they'd taken from Sawyer Brown's people, from James himself.

The others cowered, instantly afraid. James approached

Mark with his hands up. "Can I ask what this is about? We have nothing for you to take."

"What?" Mark asked, then realized what it looked it. "No!" He went from person to person, shaking their hands, but they still wouldn't look at him.

Mark was ashamed because not long ago, he would have reveled in that kind of response from the populace, but Terry Henry had shown him a better way. And if Terry got wind that they were trying to intimidate the population, he would have their asses.

Mark preferred a slap on the back to a punch in the face from the one they called "iron hands." Getting hit by Terry or Char felt like getting hit by sledgehammer.

Terry could have ruled through fear, but the lessons in pain that he delivered toughened the men, taught them a little at how to fight, and helped them better understand.

"We just want to pass the word that tomorrow, we're going to interview people who would like to join the Force de Guerre, the FDG. If anyone is interested," Mark pointed over to his left, "Terry will conduct the interviews in that small building right over there. We'd like four or five more people in the Force, that's all. Think about it and if anyone is interested, be there tomorrow morning," Mark concluded and wished them well as they shuffled past.

Mark had looked at James the whole time because the young man had nodded excessively during the short speech.

James committed to being the first one in line. He knew some others would be interested, but no one wanted it more than he did. Mark wished them well and sent them on their way.

When the small group arrived at the greenhouse, they were each given a warm breakfast roll topped with homemade jam. The others sat in silence, eating with dark expressions as they looked around the people.

That was when James snapped.

He pointed to the people and half hissed, half yelled. "Listen here, you dumb fucks! We've been given a new chance at life, a chance to actually make something of ourselves, and you sit there like you're waiting for the gallows. Well, fuck off! Stop being idiots and try to do something nice for someone else. Look at everything they're doing for us? Did Sawyer motherfucking Brown ever give you a freshly baked roll? NO!" James finished by screaming the last word, incensed at their attitudes.

He kept going as he stood up at the table waving his roll at them. "No one is going to beat you! No one is going to take anything from you. Now stop moping and start living. Otherwise, why don't you just march your happy asses into the Wastelands. What's the sense in living if you're only going to just exist? I want more, and they are making that possible. We are in a better place now, so act like it!" James stopped his tirade, looked down at his hand and stuffed the last of the roll in his mouth and stormed off.

The others were cowed by the outburst from the usually calm and pleasant young man.

The woman, Nima, stood up and looked at the others.

"What are we so unhappy about?" she asked. "I feared for my life in Brownsville and being a woman there wasn't easy, ever," she choked, barely able to get the words out. "Terry and his people have shown us nothing but kindness. My new life starts today!" she exclaimed, tipping her chin back and holding her head high.

"Even though I'm scarred, both inside and out, you tell me who isn't? If we weren't tough enough, then we wouldn't have made it to this point in time, to be here, eating a warm roll that someone else made for us, just because. Yesterday is as dead as Sawyer Brown." She spit on the ground, then stomped on it, crushing it into the dirt. She thrust a fist in the air triumphantly.

Terry and Char watched from the back door. He'd come early since he wanted to talk with James, but didn't want to interrupt the others as they talked among themselves and pledged their commitment to a better life.

One by one, the others spit and stomped on the dirt, finalizing their pact. Terry finally joined them, waving James to him. The young man ran back to the small group.

"I want to thank the nice people who run this greenhouse for everything they do. Because you help them, they have time to help you. And with that, we all benefit. Today is a new day with the whole world in front of us," Terry said, looking from face to face. "We can't go there by ourselves, and I was hoping that you'd join us. It's going to be a great ride."

Terry nodded to them, before pulling James aside.

"I like your passion," he told the young man. "You were there on the road that day Sawyer came to visit New Boulder, weren't you?"

"Yes, sir, I was covering the rear, thank god, otherwise I'd be dead along with everyone else who challenged you," James replied in a low voice, looking down.

"I just wanted to know, that's all. I blame Sawyer Brown, not you," Terry told the young man. Watching him carefully for his reaction to Char. He didn't show any fear.

"What did you see that day?" Terry pressed. Even though Char could hear them clearly from across the greenhouse, she joined them to look into the man's eyes, know the truth of what he would say.

"Not much, the horses were in the way. It started with you,

ma'am, when you jumped up and punched the boss in the face. I've never seen speed or strength like that before. Then the others fell from their horses one by one. All of a sudden Sawyer Brown was riding the other way, running for his life. If he couldn't stand up to you, who was I to stay and fight?" James looked sincere. The answer to Terry's question was that James didn't see Char turn into a Werewolf during the fight.

Their secret was safe.

Terry nodded, "I watched how you helped us bring the people from Brownsville here, and the farmer told me how you fixed his pump. I want you with us, James. I want you in the Force." Terry had wasted enough time between the FDG's last excursion and getting ready for the next one. He needed to make things happen, and most importantly, he liked making his own luck, just in case James hadn't thought about volunteering.

"Yes, sir! I'll be the first one in line for the interviews tomorrow," James replied. Terry started to laugh. James's mirth disappeared.

"James, that *was* your interview. Welcome aboard." Terry held out his hand and James took it, firmly shaking to demonstrate his strength. Terry squeezed hard enough to let James know that he had a ways to go. "Come along, we have some things we need to do."

James absently scratched Clyde's neck as he and the dog followed Terry and Char, out of the greenhouse and headed west, where they deposited James with the other four and told them to make James feel welcome, tell him the expectations, and make sure that both newcomers and old residents both knew about the interviews.

Terry needed to talk with Billy Spires about the future of New Boulder.

❖ ❖ ❖

The hunters headed into the mountains. They carried rifles that Billy had given them specifically for hunting, and they used their limited ammunition sparingly. They hunted as a team because it was more efficient. They needed to provide as much meat as possible for each bullet used since they needed to feed the whole community. These men were happy to hunt, much happier than if they'd been turned into farmers.

The hunters liked the fast pace, the glory of the kill, and for their own egos, they enjoyed being armed when most others weren't. They didn't care to be in the security force as they preferred nature over mankind. They got some of what they wanted, and they gave back to the community. Everybody won.

They headed into a valley that they hunted every couple months. They'd usually flush a herd of deer and sometimes even elk. They'd get at least one, but usually more.

The plan was that two of the men would ride to the far end of a long valley without upsetting any of the wildlife. Then they'd hunt their way downhill, driving game before them, into a trap where the third man would get clear shots at the fleeing animals.

The man with the steadiest hand stayed at the mouth of the valley as the other two headed to a higher elevation, to walk the ridge line before dipping down at the far end. They rode their horses through the pine trees, uphill, taking frequent breaks to keep the animals fresh. If they ran across a bear, the horses would need to be able to run, just in case.

The horses started to whinny and buck, but the riders didn't know why.

The Werewolves had moved to point on the ridge

overlooking the approaching horses and riders. Marcus stayed still, calm, ready to engage, but where there had once been three, there were only two. Marcus backed the Weres into heavier foliage, to hide, but the horses sensed the Were presence.

Marcus wanted to know where the other man had gone before rushing into the attack.

The hunters spurred their horses forward, talking with them to calm them down. The humans suspected a bear was nearby, so they held their rifles ready, watching the brush.

As the horses passed the Werewolves, they bolted and were soon lost in the trees toward the upper end of the valley. The horses calmed quickly once they could no longer sense a threat. The hunters continued with their plan, hoping that the spooked horses hadn't prematurely driven any game away.

They separated and covered more ground as they entered the valley and rode heavily downward, looking for any signs of game. They'd whistle a signal to their comrade who would know what to watch out for. A small herd of does flushed from a stand of pines where they'd been sleeping in the soft needles. The deer ran haphazardly down the valley. One man whistled a long steady tone, followed by five short notes. He repeated that three times. Five deer coming your way was the message.

Marcus waved the pack forward, and they flowed silently from their hiding place, downhill, blending with the shadows as they headed to intercept the men coming from their left.

The alpha heard the whistle and knew that it was a signal. The other man must have been at the mouth of the valley. A rifle fired up ahead, then a second shot. Timmons and Merrit raced forward and leapt. A horse screamed. A rifle fired three more times and went silent.

The second horse was fleeing in panic. The other Were-wolves--the bitches, Ted, and Adams--ran after it, howling in the chase. Marcus was furious. He reached out and sensed a man too far away to be caught. The man turned his horse and ran as fast as the beast could go.

A scream. The second horse went down. The rider never fired a shot. Marcus ran, saw his pack muzzle deep in prime horse flesh. He growled as he passed, barking at them to follow. Sue and Ted bounced up and charged after their alpha. The others were slower and disappeared behind Marcus as he strained the extent of his body's abilities to run faster, ever faster.

But the man was gone. His lead had been too great. The man was in the open and pounding fast toward the town of New Boulder.

The pack had been seen and they didn't look like any wolves that the man might have seen before. But he couldn't know that they were Were. Marcus held onto that thought. If he'd exposed the pack for what they were, the Forsaken would be angry.

And no one wanted to make a Vampire angry.

He looked at Ted and Sue, fire burning behind his yellow eyes. "Bring me the heads of those two fucking idiots. RIGHT NOW!" he howled.

CHAPTER FIVE

Billy sat in his chair at the table where Terry had first met him. The smaller man sat, arms crossed, and looked at the two people sitting across from him. They mirrored his pose, arms crossed and leaned back. Felicity sprawled in a loveseat against the wall, snickering.

No one had said anything yet. They all wondered what the posturing was about. Finally, Char broke the ice.

"What the hell is going on?" she blurted.

"I don't know what's going on, so , maybe you should tell me what's going on, unless there's nothing going on, and you should probably tell me that, too," Billy parried, trying not to smile.

"What?" Char curled her lip as she spoke.

"I'm not upset about anything," Terry stated. "I just wanted to talk about taking the Force into the Wasteland, look for more survivors and bring them home to New Boulder. That's all. What's up your ass, Billy?"

"Nothing. You come storming in here like you own the place, of course I think you're up to something," Billy said as he unfolded his arms, rolled out the middle finger of both hands, and thrust them into the air in Terry's direction.

"Well, Billy Spires, I thank you for declaring that I'm number one! It is an honor that I've worked long and hard to achieve. I must say, however, that you and I have very different ideas about what "storming in" entails. In any case, I'd like to work our way up to ten people in the Force and keep building from there. We're expanding, Billy, and for that, we need people to feel safe and secure. We need the manpower to grow."

"I can't disagree with that. How much do you think we can grow before New Boulder becomes too small?"

Terry shrugged. He could have answered with something, but for this one, it was Billy's call.

"I think we'll know it when we see it, but that's a long ways off. Until then, let's see what she'll handle. What's your plan for the new people, train them while you're on the road?" Billy asked.

"A mix–leave Mark and Ivan here, take Jim and Devlin with us. We'll split the new people between us. That'll give us a couple extra horses to take as well, leaving the rest here. You'll have some people and firepower in New Boulder, while we have everything we need with us. I think it's a good balance between offensive and defensive use of the FDG." They continued to talk through the logistics, while intermittently, Terry would give Billy the finger and vice versa.

Char had plenty of the male bonding stuff with the pack. She shook her head, she understood it, and although she never saw any utility in it, she tolerated it.

Barely.

❖ ❖ ❖

Blaine stayed low in the saddle, riding as if the hounds of hell were on his heels. The horse frothed, pounding the old pavement as it raced south toward New Boulder. The hunter kept looking over his shoulder, expecting to see the wolves at any moment, running with their unnatural speed after him. He thought they were as large as the horses his two friends rode. They'd attacked mercilessly and seemed immune to getting shot.

He had turned the horse and fled from the ambush site, where the men thought they were the predators, but discovered they were the prey.

Blaine didn't slow until he passed the power plant. He continued to ride toward the mayor's house, without acknowledging anyone he saw along the way.

He slowed just enough to jump from the horse. It continued trotting away until it found a patch of grass to eat. Blaine ran through the front door and without hesitation, barreled into Billy's study.

Char leapt to the side, turning and crouching in a single move. One of her Glock pistols appeared in her hand, aimed at the intruder. Terry went the other way, rolling and coming up with his bullwhip ready. In his other hand, he gripped a knife by the blade. Blaine froze and held his hands up.

The sudden silence was interrupted by Terry's comment. "I might call that 'storming in,' for future reference," he said, putting his knife away and coiling the whip to hang it back from his belt. Char relaxed, but kept her pistol pointed at the hunter. Clyde barked, hackles raised.

"Out with it!" Billy yelled. "Before she shoots your dumb ass."

"I ain't seen nothin' like it. Fucking wolves the size of horses attacked us, killed Eric and Trash! They didn't even hesitate, howled into the valley, ran down a horse at full gallop as if it were nothin'!" the man whined, his hand constantly moving back and forth on the top of his head.

Char turned sheet white and carefully holstered her pistol.

"Wolves the size of horses? What the hell are you smoking?" Billy replied. "Get a grip, Blaine. There's no such thing."

Blaine staggered to the chair that Terry had previously occupied and fell heavily into it. The whites of his eyes showed as he struggled on the edge of panic.

"I'm not smoking anything, Billy. My friends are dead. Killed by those creatures." Blaine sighed and put his head down on the table.

Billy replied, "I think this is a job for the FDG. Take your boys up there and see if you can find them, recover what's left, the rifles and ammo, especially. Determine what killed them." Billy hesitated and looked closer into Terry's green eyes. "You think it was the same that killed our other man?"

Terry looked from Billy to Char and back to Billy. "Could be. Don't know until I take a look, but I'm not in a hurry to go that way, if you know what I mean. Blaine, you said they ran down a horse at a gallop. How'd you get away?"

"I was at the other end of the valley, could seem 'em through a break in the trees. They was a long ways off, but I seen it all! Ran soon as it happened. No sense in all of us dyin', then's you wouldn't a' known what happened," he said defensively.

"No one's questioning your manliness, Blaine. Seeing what you saw, any right-minded person would have run. Tomorrow, we'll take a look, and we need you to show us where you were," Terry soothed, but Blaine started shaking his head and mumbling.

"Char? Are you okay?" Billy asked. Felicity sat wide-eyed, unsure of what to think. Clyde started barking again. "I didn't take you for being squeamish."

"It's not that. I think it was something I ate," she suggested as the color slowly returned to her face. Her purple eyes blazed with an internal fire that concerned Terry. Char's pack had returned, and she was afraid.

❖ ❖ ❖

Marcus slowly walked back up the valley. He was trying to control his rage, but failing. He passed the nearest bunch as they were gorging on the horse. He growled and snapped at them, his massive hackles raised, his head looming above them. They cowered and moved aside for the alpha.

He walked past the horse to the man, dead from a broken neck. Marcus pawed the rifle away, then reared and dove in, biting deeply into the man's abdomen. He pulled back, entrails spilling from his muzzle. He threw his head back, gulping down a chunk of the man's coat along with skin, muscle, and guts. The other Werewolves watched in horror, hoping that he wouldn't demand they partake.

He didn't.

Marcus cracked the man's ribs with his fearsome jaws, tore them away, and pulled out the heart. He chewed it slowly, his eyes closed. He breathed deeply of the cool, pine-scented air. There was one more man and one more heart to be eaten. Maybe he wouldn't kill Timmons and Merrit.

Marcus strutted away, savoring the coppery aftertaste of that which made a man what he was.

He continued up the valley, feeling better as he went. The rest of his pack followed, appropriately submissive, at a respectful distance. When Marcus reached the site of the first kill, he found his two errant Wolves, injured and back in human form. They had eaten some of the horse, but they were both in agony from bullet wounds. Timmons was missing part of his shoulder where one round had ripped through. Merrit kept pressure on the two bullet holes in his chest.

Marcus was pleased that they were injured, pleased that they weren't dead, and impressed that they were able to bring down the man and the horse while so severely wounded.

He wouldn't tell them that.

Marcus changed into human form, "You fuckwits blew the whole thing!" he growled. "Serves you right to get fucked up. Quit your crying and get yourselves straight." Marcus stepped on them on his way to the human.

The man was pinned beneath the horse, a gash on his head where he'd been slammed on the ground. His eyes looked up, but they were unfocused.

"You're still alive? Well now, won't this be a special treat." Marcus dug through the hunter's things until he found a knife. He cut away the man's jacket and shirt. With a cry of rage, he plunged the knife into the man's chest, slicing through the cartilage between the ribs above and below the heart. He reached his hand into the cut, grasped the ribs and yanked outward, tearing them away from the still beating heart. He reached in, grabbed and twisted, then pulled it out, biting into it with his human teeth, ripping a chunk out, and chewing it as blood ran down his chin, staring at the man's eyes as they faded out.

If Werewolves could look pale, they did. Sue changed into human form and turned away so she could throw up in peace. The others sat and watched, wondering how far they'd fallen to get to this point. And none of them were strong enough to do anything about it.

Not alone, anyway.

❖ ❖ ❖

"What are we doing here?" Char asked as Terry entered the small building, found the table, and sat down behind it. It was dark inside, but he could see, as could Char.

"Getting ready to conduct the interviews, why?" he asked innocently.

"Aren't we supposed to check on the hunters?"

"I'm not in any hurry to go up there. Are you?" Terry looked closely at her, wanting to see what she didn't say. Terry was an expert in reading body language. It gave him an edge, always, put him one heartbeat ahead of his opponents. And usually that was all he needed.

Char gave nothing away. "Not really," was all she said.

"Mark!" he yelled. The man he'd promoted to corporal entered, stopping at the doorway and squinting into the darkness. "When are the victims going to show?"

"Looks like they were waiting on you before making their move. I think we've got a group coming right now," Mark told them as he stood tall, a spring in his step.

Terry examined the man, who had recently been a town bully, thanks to that worthless scumbag John. Killing that man in front of the others made the right impression. Giving Mark a chance had been the right decision, too. Mark was going to be a good addition to the FDG, and he'd help build it into something they could all be proud of.

"Send in Devlin and James, please," Terry said casually.

"Have the volunteers wait out there until I call for them."

Devlin and James entered, stopping at the doorway as Mark had. "Come on in, Privates! It'll help your eyes adjust more quickly if you're in the darkness. Stop! You almost ran into the table. Now, here's what we're going to do…"

Terry outlined the plan to the two men. Char shook her head, but stood back against the wall, out of the way. She didn't know what her role was in all this, but felt like she needed to watch over TH, just in case the pack made an untimely appearance.

Devlin stood in the shadows on one side of the room and James in the shadows on the other. Terry leaned back in the chair. It creaked under his weight. Dust floated within two beams of light, shining through holes in the roof. It smelled musty. Char sneezed, whispering an apology, then wondered why she was whispering.

"Mark!" Terry bellowed. "Send in the first two victims!"

Two rough men opened the door and stepped into the darkness. Terry looked like a statue, barely visible as he sat behind the rough-hewn table.

"Why should I bring you on board?" he asked in a low voice, raspy from eating too much dust.

"We're the last of the Marines," one of the two offered.

"Like fuck you are. You look like dick-less wonders to me," Terry countered.

"Stand up and say that to my face, asshole!" the second of the pair spat toward Terry's dark figure.

Their eyes were not yet adjusted from the Wasteland sun, and they didn't see that they weren't alone. The shadow nodded to Devlin, who rotated and swung a fist, catching one of the two applicants in the abdomen. He folded over and rolled to the floor.

"Hey!" the other shouted, but he froze in place as his eyes darted wildly about. The punch from the second man dropped him like a sack of feed grain. The shadow of a man stood and threw the table to the side, stepping forward and crouching.

"You *are* a dick-less wonder, asshole," he said to the man's face. "Now let's see if there's a fighter within that worthless hide of yours, a fighter that is useful to the Force de Guerre."

The interviews were less congenial to some, based on their approaches. In the end, Terry selected five men and one woman, hoping that at least five would make the grade.

He wanted all six.

When he lined the newcomers up, he didn't like what he saw. He scowled darkly. "Names!" he yelled. No one moved. Terry pulled his bullwhip and snapped it between the first two in line. He pulled it back and recoiled it. He liked the snakeskin grip he'd made for the handle. It made the grip a little larger and felt better in his hand.

Mark stepped in, trying to be the good Marine as a balance to Terry's tough Marine. He pointed to the first recruit, "Tell him your name," he moved his finger to the second person, "then you and so on down the line."

Boris and David were brothers, the first two into the interview. Charlie and Lacy were the next two, and the final pair were two unlikely looking candidates, young and small in stature. Sawyer Brown had called one of those Asswipe, and he was the young man who worked as a personal servant to the big man. The other had worked in the stable. They said they didn't have names, only what they were called in Brownsville.

"So, you want me to give you a Force de Guerre nickname?" Terry asked, liking the situation. Instead of pity, all he saw was a new world in front of the two young men and he was happy to welcome them into it.

"You will be known as Blackbeard. If you don't know who he was, he was a pirate," he told the man who had yet to grow any facial hair, the one called Asswipe. "And you, we'll call you Geronimo, after a great warrior from the before time who was one with both the horses and the land. Blackie, Geronimo, welcome aboard. Now get on your faces and push that dirt down." None of them moved.

Terry clenched his fists for a moment before pulling out his bullwhip. His men jumped into the ranks, forced the newcomers onto the ground, and showed them the front-leaning rest, the pushup position.

Char snickered from behind the group. Terry pointed to her and then to the ground. She mouthed the word "nope" and strolled away.

CHAPTER SIX

Marcus was perched on the rock overlooking New Boulder. The rest of the pack was gathered around, watching their alpha. They had been living in fear for a long time. The first incident when they arrived put them on edge, but yesterday's sent them over.

Horror didn't begin to describe it. Werewolves didn't eat people. Period. That wasn't true anymore, was it?

"We need to go down there, check on Char..." Marcus said. It wasn't a question, and he wasn't talking to any of the pack. He didn't need their permission. He told them what to do, and they did it.

It was the way of the Were.

"There's nothing right about this place, Marcus," Sue offered. She was a small She-Wolf, so Marcus didn't give her as hard a time as any of the males. "I think we need to keep moving. You go get Char, and then we'll all leave this place."

The others cringed, waiting for the alpha's inevitable emotional eruption and subsequent tirade.

But it didn't come. He only nodded. "I think you're right, Sue. I need my mate. Wait here," he ordered as he vaulted the rocks, then jumped and ran downhill, much the same way Char had done so long ago.

❖ ❖ ❖

Blaine was on his horse, but sat, paralyzed with fear. He was almost catatonic. Terry casually rode past and took the reins from the man's hand. He pulled Blaine's horse behind his own, while Char rode by his side and Clyde ran ahead.

After riding slowly for an hour, Blaine still hadn't talked. Char wondered why they were bringing him. Even after two days, she figured she would be able to spot the place where the horse galloped from the hills.

Terry kicked his horse into a trot, pulling Blaine's horse up to speed as Char ran her horse forward. Clyde raced her for a while, then gave up and turned to sniffing a bush that would inevitably get peed on. Terry turned from watching the dog as he saw Char waving. She had stopped and turned sideways in the old road.

Blaine started to whimper and shake. Terry let go, waving the hunter away. The man was immediately energized, swinging around the horse to grab the reins and turn south, where he spurred his horse into a run.

Terry couldn't blame the man. He'd seen something your average human was never meant to see. Blaine's punishment was that he'd live the rest of his life with that vision.

Terry pitied the man.

Char pointed the way ahead. Terry didn't want to go first.

There was a minor stalemate.

"What's the problem? Big, tough Marine afraid of some bad doggies?" she prodded.

"Are they up there?" Terry asked.

"How would I know?" she countered.

"Werewolves can sense their own kind. So, I'll ask you again, are they up there?"

She stared at him without blinking, a yellow glint behind the purple. He could almost see the Werewolf behind that beautiful face, sizing him up for her next kill.

Her mind worked, until she realized that he'd known all along. *How could I have missed that?* she wondered.

"What is your claim to fame, Terry Henry Walton? You aren't what you seem either, if we're being candid. Nanocytes?" she asked.

"Only because I had no choice, but they've come in handy." They sat on their horses, looking at each other. Two master chess players, neither willing to give away their next move. Clyde started braying and ran into the brush.

"I have to trust that you're not leading me into a trap," he finally admitted.

"They're not in that valley or anywhere near here. Actually, I can't tell where they are," she said. Terry looked for cues that she might be lying, but could find none. He saw nothing in her body language that suggested she was telling the truth either. He was stumped.

"I guess if you wanted, I'd be dead already, wouldn't I?" he asked.

"I'm not so sure about that, TH. I've never met a man who could fight like you. I need you to keep teaching me. I need to be the best there ever was." The purple in her eyes seemed to swirl. Terry felt like he was looking into the cosmos. He blinked to make sure she wasn't using a Werewolf mind trick on him.

Could Werewolves do Jedi mind tricks? Terry wasn't too sure, he never asked enough questions when he had the chance.

But, he found he could look away if he wanted. Her eyes were just doing their own thing.

He liked watching it.

"That's a lofty goal, Char," he finally answered.

"It's the goal I have. So, are we going to go up there, find the remains of the men, scavenge a few things, and then get the hell out of there?"

"I guess we should. I'll go first. I don't know why, but I trust you. I trust a fucking Werewolf. By the way, since I know, aren't you supposed to kill me now?" he asked, smiling playfully.

"We're allowed to keep pets, so I've claimed you and Clyde. I hope you don't mind?" Terry shook his head, slowly, wondering if she was kidding or not.

"What do we have to fear from the pack?" Terry asked over his shoulder as he nosed his horse into the brush to follow Blaine's trail.

"Judging by what we find up ahead, probably a great deal," Char replied.

Terry looked at the valley before him as he rode unerringly toward it. The sense of doom was overwhelming, and Terry didn't know why. He believed that the Werewolves had moved on. He shook his head as if that would help.

It didn't.

They'd shared their secrets. They'd both known, but neither trusted the other enough to be open. They'd dodged and parried, but now that they knew...

What would change between them?

And that was what darkened Terry's mood. He didn't want

anything to change between he and Char. He'd grown used to having her counsel and her heightened senses nearby. He also found it comforting to have one of the deadliest fighters he'd ever known on his team. He considered himself in the elite category, but Char's speed and unnatural strength gave her an edge unmatched by any normal man, even one enhanced such as himself.

And then there was the healing that both he and Char enjoyed. Which reminded him, now that he could ask.

"They shot you, didn't they?"

"What are you talking about?" she asked in reply.

"When we fought with Sawyer Brown's men. You went off by yourself and the next time I saw you, you had two bullet holes in your clothes," he clarified.

"Well, of course they shot me, but they didn't hit anything important. I think they shot you, too, didn't they?"

"Yes, but in my case, they did hit something important. That bastard shot my .45. Thank you for bringing up such a painful topic!" He gave her his best angry look.

"Me being shot wasn't as painful as losing that stupid pistol. Is that what I just heard come out of your mouth?" She urged her mount forward so she could ride alongside Terry in order to give him her own angry look.

Terry checked his rifle and wouldn't look at her.

"You know that won't help, right?" she asked.

"Silver bullet, in the head? I think it'll put a hurt on them." He wasn't sure what she was after.

"They are my people, and they are my friends," Char whispered.

Terry stopped, forcing Char to stop and turn, "And they are killing my people. Whatever we need to do to stop that, I'm going to do. Just let me know what it is. Why did you come into town Char? What's your game?"

She thought about it, then decided that she didn't want to lie. "To check you out. Find out if the town was going to be a threat. They'll want to know that you aren't a danger to them. That's what I'll tell them, anyway," she offered.

"Are you going to leave us?" he asked, instantly unhappy at the thought.

She paused, "I don't think so, not yet. Clyde would miss me, wouldn't you, boy?" Clyde had rejoined them from his foray into the brush and was jogging along happily between the two horses.

Terry simply nodded. His ears perked up. "You said they weren't here," he growled angrily as he heard a snort and growl from the trees ahead.

"Bear," she replied.

"What?"

"Bear... A BEAR!" she yelled as the large black bear broke cover and scampered toward them. Terry snap fired, then aimed and fired five more times. The bear ploughed ahead, even though Terry was certain he'd hit what he was aiming at. The horse pranced as the bear closed the last ten yards.

A pistol cracked once, twice beside him and the bear rolled in a heap. A smoke tendril escaped the barrel of Char's Glock. Terry climbed down from his horse and checked the bear.

Both eyes had been shot out.

Most of his rounds had skipped off the bear's skull. Two rounds had hit the bear in the chest and would have eventually killed it, but not before it had mauled both the horses and the humans.

"You've been practicing," Terry said, still looking at the bear.

"Maybe I was a good shot before," she suggested, smiling.

"I'm sorry, Char. I'm sorry I thought you tricked me, fed me to the wolves, as it may be." He turned to look at her for a moment, "But that wouldn't be a very nice thing to do to your pet, now would it?" Terry examined the bear, looking for anything odd, but no. It was just a large black bear.

"No worries, TH. It's you and me and against the world, isn't it?" Char asked, leaning forward in her saddle, purple eyes sparkling.

Terry hung his head, then turned his attention to the valley spreading before them. "I have two friends in this world. One is an old lady who beats me with her wooden spoon and the other is a Werewolf. What in the holy jump the fuck up and down is my world coming to?" He finished looking around before continuing. "Let's go find the hunters and then be on our way. I bet if we backtrack the bear, we'll find something. And we're coming back for that," he stated, pointing to the bear and nodding. "Black bear is some good eating!"

"I know, but you'll want to cook it, won't you?" Char toyed with him.

"If you want, I can go ahead and you can stay here and snack a bit. Don't think I hadn't noticed how much damn venison you've been eating. Have you seen Margie Rose looking at me? She thinks I'm the one sneaking it in the middle of the night."

Char held her finger to her lips. "Shhhh."

She waved TH forward and they both headed into the valley, climbing as they passed through the thinning pines. Hills turned into mountains. It would have been a pleasant place had the circumstances been different.

The smell was obvious and not far away.

CHAPTER SEVEN

Marcus hit the pavement at the edge of town and slowed to a walk. He strolled casually, looking at the variety of buildings still standing but unoccupied. He stopped and closed his eyes, sniffing the air, reaching out with his senses.

So many people.

Wildlife even. Horses. But no Werewolves. "Where are you, Charumati? Where the hell did you get off to?" Marcus asked the sky. "I guess that I'll have to ask someone, you fucking bitch! I hate asking humans anything. I can't wait to get my paws on you, teach you some manners."

Marcus fumed as he walked toward the center of the small town. He smelled the power plant and it reminded him of long ago, of New York City, where he'd lived most of his life. He even spent some time as a stock broker. The others never had a chance with him on the trading floor. The other traders thought they were cutthroat, but they had no idea what that term really meant.

Civilization. He longed for it. His descent toward barbarism was his way of dealing with the absence, but what if?

"Maybe the whole pack needs to come here. Timmons is an engineer by trade, could probably help them get up to speed more quickly. And then nightlife. Booze. Music. Fun. Sonofabitch," he cried. "None of that stuff is coming back. Two seconds after I find you, Char, we're leaving this place. Let the humans wither and die in this hell hole." Marcus stomped his feet and stormed around in a circle. His fists were clenched and his jaw started to ache from clenching it so hard.

He yelled at the sky, then continued walking. He meandered until he found someone.

"Excuse me, is there someone in charge here that I could talk with? I've only recently arrived and need to get my bearings," Marcus said pleasantly, while his yellow eyes glared at the young man before him.

Unnerved, the man didn't speak. He only pointed to a nondescript house not far away.

"Thank you," Marcus added as an afterthought, having already walked away, making a beeline for the indicated place.

When he arrived, he knocked on the door and waited. Then he knocked harder, almost pounding on the door. When it opened, the initially angry face quickly transformed into a radiant smile as the beautiful woman looked up at him.

In human form, Marcus was a beast, towering toward six feet eight inches and built like a professional wrestler. His massive frame was topped with short black hair. He had bushy eyebrows under which his yellow eyes peered. He held out a hand into which Felicity's dainty counterpart disappeared.

"I'm looking for someone in charge. I've just arrived and

have some questions." Marcus smiled graciously. He wouldn't mind adding this one to his stable. It had been a while since he'd had a human woman, usually they couldn't handle his vigor, but this one seemed to glow with a certain energy.

He'd consider it.

"You'll want to talk with Billy Spires," she drawled slowly as she looked him up and down. It had been a long time since anyone showed such appreciation. "I didn't get your name, handsome stranger?"

"I'm Marcus. And you, beautiful stranger?"

"Felicity, and my, you are something. Follow me," she said, swinging her hips as she turned and headed inside.

"My pleasure," Marcus flirted, feeling a little of his old self returning.

Felicity made a show of opening the door to the study and smiled seductively as he made his way past her, locking eyes with the smaller man at the other end of the table. Marcus trailed a finger along Felicity's arm as he squeezed by her in the doorway. He felt her shiver.

Good.

He'd never taken his eyes from the man she'd called Billy Spires.

Billy looked back through narrowed eyes, trying not to be intimidated by the immense being who had just walked into his office.

Marcus pulled a chair from the table, spun it around, and sat on it backwards as Terry Henry often did.

"Billy dear, this is Marcus. He's newly arrived and has some questions for you."

"Leave us. Close the door on your way out," Billy ordered, ice forming on every word. Felicity hesitated for only a moment, scowling darkly at Billy from behind the safety of the newcomer. She left and gently closed the door, hoping that Marcus appreciated her dignity and grace.

❖ ❖ ❖

TH took a knee next to the remains of the hunter. There was almost nothing left of the horse beside him. At least it was cool enough that the stench wasn't overwhelming.

Terry looked at how the man's chest had been torn apart by the jaws of an animal and noticed the bear's tracks around in the dirt. "This wasn't our bear, was it?"

Terry could see that the wound wasn't fresh.

Char had turned a milky shade of white as she looked at the body. She leaned closer and sniffed.

Were saliva. Marcus's saliva. None of the others. They had eaten the horse, but only Marcus had eaten the man.

"The alpha, my mate, he did this." Terry's lip curled in disgust thinking of Char with a Werewolf that would stoop to tearing out a human's heart.

"The pack ate the horse. Let's find the other. I can smell him, up ahead." Terry sniffed and couldn't smell anything except the rotting remains of the man and horse at his feet. Terry found the rifle a few feet away and some loose shells. They recovered their horses, tied a short distance away because the animals shied at the smell of death.

Terry and Char rode forward quickly, stopping when they got close, and for a second time tied off the horses. This site was different as it had not been disturbed by the bear.

Char sniffed the area and walked around it like a crime scene investigator. "Were blood. I suspect the hunter shot one of the pack, maybe two. The blood is old and mixed with the horse." She smelled puke, not far off. Sue. Finally she kneeled next to the man, with Terry leaning over her shoulder. They both studied the injury to the man's chest. A knife wound, followed by ripping and tearing. The heart had been pulled out.

Char cried gently, her shoulders drooping as she hung her head. Clyde nuzzled her with his hackles raised. He could smell the Were strangers, and he didn't like it.

"He changed into a human and ate this man's heart like that, one man eating another. This is the most disgusting thing I've ever seen, ever even heard of." She choked out the words.

"And that answers my question. This isn't normal. What the fuck do we do, Char?" Terry couldn't look at the man's remains and not feel fear.

He turned to the mundane, digging the man's rifle out from beneath his body. He didn't find any extra ammunition. The bolt of the hunting rifle was locked back, showing an empty chamber. Were blood. At least the man went down fighting. "Fucking A, my friend." Terry said, "Fight back with all you have."

Terry assumed the position of attention and saluted the man. Char didn't understand.

"He's dead," she said simply.

He slowly dropped his salute, "And he died as a warrior, fighting past his last bullet. He deserves to be honored. It is the least we can do for him, because I'm not staying here to bury him. He'll be food for the birds, the scavengers, until his bones disappear into the ground in the decades ahead," Terry replied, returning to his horse to stash the rifle with the other. "Let's recover that bear. We still need to eat, and I want that hide as a rug in Margie Rose's living room. That floor is going to be cold this winter."

Char started to smile as if she had a good comeback, but then looked at the mess her mate had left behind, reminded of the mess that he'd become, and it sickened her. Terry put a hand on her back and rubbed gently, feeling that her muscles were tighter than usual.

"Come on, Char. We have stuff to do and none of it is here…"

❖ ❖ ❖

Felicity stayed outside the door, listening as Marcus wove an elaborate tale of his storied past, of travels through the mountains, following the elk for food. And then he dropped the big one.

He'd become separated from his wife and wondered if she'd made her way into town, a tall woman with purple eyes.

Felicity's jaw hit the floor. She couldn't see, but suspected that Billy was equally shocked. *Why, that little vixen never mentioned a husband, and a strapping one at that*, Felicity thought.

Billy recovered quicker than Felicity.

"Why yes, she showed up quite a while ago. She is safe, as my security chief is protecting her," Billy said, trying to be diplomatic. Despite Terry's denials, Billy was convinced there was something going on between those two. But he had just grown accustomed to Terry Henry and didn't want to lose him. There was no way anyone could survive a fight with the monster that sat at the other end of Billy's table.

"I hope you are pleased that she is quite safe and healthy. She's been an important part of our community ever since she arrived, even helping us immensely with an issue regarding our neighbors to the south," Billy said cryptically, not wanting to offend the man by telling him they had put her on the front lines of their battle with Sawyer Brown. That kind of protection would not be well received, Billy expected.

"She is always so helpful. If you can tell me where she is, then I'd like to collect her, and we'll be on our way."

Collect her, Felicity repeated to herself, liking the big man less and less by the moment.

"She's not here right now. They took two horses and went north, to check out a new hunting ground up that way," Billy said, smiling to put Marcus at ease, but the big man's yellow eyes narrowed and his brow furled. His lip quivered as it turned into a snarl.

"When will they be back?" he growled.

Billy was under no illusions that he could defend himself from this man. Billy had grown used to Terry Henry's presence and had stopped bringing a firearm into the room where he met with the townspeople. He was unarmed and faced a man easily twice his size.

"I don't know," Billy said, barely above a whisper.

Marcus closed his eyes and breathed deeply. He could smell the female just outside the door. Her pheromones had changed from intensely sensual to fear.

Pity.

When he opened his eyes again, he had calmed himself. No better place to wait than with the man who seemed to know what was going on. "Tell me about this place. How did you come to build such a civilization from the ruins of the world? You have electricity! You should be proud of yourself, Billy Spires, for what you've accomplished. I'd like to hear more, if you would be so kind."

Billy hesitated, but started with his early life. It had been a while since he told anyone the stories. They weren't very impressive. He survived and that was that, but this was an opportunity to embellish, work on his legacy as the first mayor, governor, maybe even president in this new world. Once Billy got rolling, there was no stopping him.

Felicity went upstairs, shaking her head the whole way.

❖ ❖ ❖

Terry was a madman cleaning the bear, flying through the process because he wanted to be on his way. He gutted it and cut off the head and feet, then split the beast in half. It took their combined strength to put the front half of the carcass behind one saddle, then the back half behind the other. Clyde seemed to be right at home around the bear. He nipped at it, barking and playing. He helped himself to some choice tidbits from the entrails.

"Damn dog!" Terry said, still chagrined that Clyde wouldn't taste his beer.

Char's mood hadn't changed. The darkness of what happened in that valley hung over her head like a storm cloud.

Once the bear was loaded, they rode downhill quickly, reached the road, turned right, and headed toward New Boulder at a quick trot.

"I wonder if Blaine made it back," Terry said, trying to make small talk, but Char wasn't having it. She kept her thoughts to herself as they rode toward town.

When they got close, she sat up straight and stared into the distance. "We have a problem," she groaned.

❖ ❖ ❖

Marcus listened quietly, killing time. The more Billy talked, the more Marcus wanted to eat the little man's heart. But then he felt the spark. He closed his eyes and reached out.

Char had returned.

Marcus didn't waste time with pleasantries. He stood up and walked out, leaving Billy speechless and frozen, but only for a moment.

The mayor bolted out the back door of his office, heading straight for the armory. He unlocked it and pulled his trusty rifle, the AK-74, the one that could fire the NATO rounds. He checked the magazine to ensure it was loaded, then inserted it, front first, rotating it toward the back until it seated. He pulled the bolt back, then let it go to send a round into the chamber.

Carrying the rifle before him, he walked carefully to the front door, which hung open after Marcus's hasty departure. Felicity was descending the stairs. "Get back upstairs and lock the door!" he shouted.

Felicity felt a strange sensation. Billy was going to protect her from the big man, put his small body between Marcus and her. She held her head proudly as she ran back up the stairs, into the bedroom, and locked the door behind her. She continued to the window and looked out.

Marcus stood at the street corner, looking north toward the power plant.

Billy stood on the steps below, rifle ready but not aimed. Marcus seemed oblivious to him.

CHAPTER EIGHT

Your mate?" Terry's lip curled as he said the words. Char nodded without looking in his direction. When Char moved in under Margie Rose's roof with Terry, he had taken a silver coin, melted it, and dripped the silver onto one of his knives. It was the only thing he had to defend himself from a Werewolf.

He could see Char's color change to a shade of red as the anger grew within. The horses walked at a steady pace, past the power plant and toward Billy's house.

When they spotted Marcus, Char growled, feral, bestial.

"You gotta be shitting me," Terry blurted as he saw the immense man who stood waiting for them, arms at his side, fists clenched. "Fuck me."

Clyde brayed and barked

Char didn't say anything, but stopped her horse when they were still twenty feet away. Terry felt that he sat almost eye-to-eye with the Werewolf alpha, even though he was sitting on a horse.

The bigger they are... he thought, trying to console himself. It wasn't working. Once past the initial intimidation, Terry studied the man, clinically. He had to have weaknesses.

Everyone did, even Werewolves.

"Why don't you come closer, give us a kiss, honey," Marcus said, watching the human at her side. He could sense something different about that one, but couldn't put his finger on it. Terry glared back at the big man, letting adrenaline surge into his body as it prepared itself to fight the enemy.

No one had to be an expert in body language to read Char's abject hatred for the creature before her.

They stood looking at each other before Marcus turned his attention toward the security chief. The Werewolf strolled forward with his hands up. Terry continued to cradle his M4 combat rifle.

Marcus thrust out a massive paw. Terry was torn, but with his left hand on the trigger, Terry grabbed the man's hand, a mistake he quickly learned. Marcus was the alpha and unable to do anything other than establish dominance. Terry Henry Walton was a challenger who needed to be put in his place.

Marcus brought his full power to bear in an effort to crush the human's hand. Terry fought back, gritting his teeth with his effort. The nanocytes surged into the muscles of his arm. The two achieved a minor stalemate, but that didn't last long. Terry felt his hand getting squeezed beyond his capacity to stop it.

Char leapt from her horse, moved behind Marcus in a flash, and punched him in the kidney with everything she had. He let go and turned, crouching.

Terry aimed his rifle one handed. He couldn't miss such a

large target at this close of a range. He flexed his numb right hand until he was able to pull his silvered blade. Terry Henry Walton prepared himself to dive from the horse.

Char snarled, hands up, dancing like a boxer ready to wade into the middle of the ring.

Marcus recognized the challenge, but now was not the time. He stood up and held his hands out in front of himself.

"I apologize. Sometimes I get overzealous with my size. I hope that I didn't hurt you," Marcus said, looking at Terry.

Terry Henry Walton couldn't miss the opportunity to get in a jab. He turned and looked behind himself, then pointed at his own chest. "What, me? You think you hurt me? I was going to apologize to you," he countered. "You are okay, aren't you?"

Marcus rolled his eyes. Char put her hands on her hips and glared.

"What are you doing here?" she asked sharply, accusingly.

"Just coming to pick up the love of my life so we can be on our way. So, come along now, time to go." He didn't give her any choice. She crossed her arms and stood defiantly.

"I'm not quite ready yet. You go along. I'll catch up later," she replied.

Marcus's forced smile disappeared. "I think you're ready now."

"No. And that's all I'm going to take from you. Why don't you go fuck yourself," she snapped.

"I think it's going to snow," Terry said as he eased his horse between the two Werewolves. "How about we go inside and talk about his like adults. This bear isn't getting cooked while it sits on the back of these horses. Maybe you can help carry this haunch inside, big man. I'd be grateful for the help."

"Why don't you curl yourself into a little frightened ball so

I can kick your ass out of this conversation." Marcus showed his teeth as he glowered at Terry.

"I think Charumati told you to move on, so why don't you do just that. Just because we don't want a fight doesn't mean we won't." Terry rotated his knife blade so a glint of silver flashed into the alpha's eyes.

Billy Spires had moved to the far side of the road, giving himself a clear line of fire to the newcomer. Billy aimed and held steady, then dropped to a knee as the posturing continued.

"Fuck off, asslick," Marcus growled.

A weakness, Terry told himself. *Maybe it's not the best tactic to drive a Werewolf into a rage. Nice wolfie...*

"Why don't you fuck off?" Char countered, stepping beyond the horse, who had started prancing while being so close to two angry Werewolves. Terry dismounted, stepped aside, and slapped the horse, making it run, not far, but far enough.

Terry angled away, surrounding Marcus. The alpha looked from one of his adversaries to the other, his yellow eyes fixing on Terry's silver blade. He wondered if the strange human knew he and Char were Werewolves.

He had to. Who else carried a silver weapon? Marcus sniffed toward Terry, sure that the human wasn't of the Were world, but he was different. His hand should have been crushed under Marcus's great strength.

It wasn't. Char was right, damn the bitch. It wasn't the time.

"This isn't over," he said as he straightened and slowly backed out of the circle. He turned and headed down the road toward the mountains, jogging at first, but then running, faster and faster until he hit Were speed and disappeared. Clyde ran after him for a short way, barking his dismay, but

Terry called the dog back.

Char and Terry looked at each other knowingly, while Billy remained on the outside looking in.

"What the fuck was that all about? Who in God's creation is that cockwad?" Billy asked, flustered and still aiming his rifle at the road Marcus had taken on his way from town.

"That cockwad is my ex-husband, and you can believe that he will be back. He doesn't like to lose…at anything." She remained motionless, looking toward the hills.

"Bear? It'll be good it if doesn't rot from all of us just standing here, not processing it. A little help?" Terry asked as he started to untie the carcass. Blood ran down the backs of both horses.

Terry pulled the two rifles from where he'd stuffed them between the saddle and the bear. Handing the rifles to Billy, he decided that Billy didn't need to know anything else.

Felicity finally joined the group. "Well, my dear, I see why he is your ex. That is one angry man, an angry and very large man. A shame that his ego is so fragile that he has to control you. I really feel sorry for you, Char," Felicity purred.

Char looked the smaller woman over. "If you only knew," she replied as she grabbed the bear haunch and hoisted it over a shoulder, carrying it by herself toward the back door to the kitchen. Terry accepted the challenge and took the other, grunting under the weight as he staggered through Billy's yard. Billy tied the horses to a fence post and asked Felicity to bring them water.

The mayor joined Terry and Char. "Where in the fuck did that man-mountain come from?" he demanded, grabbing Char by the arm. She whirled so fast that Billy tripped trying to step back and fell, landing heavily on his ass.

"Don't touch me, ever again," Char said in a low and dangerous voice. Billy held his hands up, before Terry helped the man to his feet.

"I didn't mean nothing by it," he mumbled. "How many fucking people are traipsing around the goddamned mountains? It's like a parade and how in the hell do they grow so big out there? Can either of you clownburgers explain any of this to me?"

"I don't know what to tell you, Billy. Thanks for backing us up out there. I expect that Marcus is probably the most dangerous man we have ever met. And you were right there with us, ready to wade into the middle of it. Damn, Billy, you are one tough ball-slapper!"

Billy blinked twice at Terry before answering, "I'm not sure if I'm supposed to be pleased by that or not," he replied.

Char looked at Terry. "You're right about that. Marcus is a killer, orders of magnitude worse than that simpering fuckwit Sawyer Brown." Char looked like she wanted to say more, but not with Billy there. He didn't need to know the secret of the mountain travelers.

Terry pulled out his knife, washed off the blade, and told the others to take care with the hide. He wanted it. Terry and Char worked methodically and butchered the bear in short order, without any conversation. Billy gave up and went outside to wash down the horses.

Billy finally found a hobby he liked: riding horses. They didn't give him grief when he talked and when he sat astride one, he could feel their power beneath him. He reveled in sharing that.

The others rode for convenience's sake. Not him.

Terry and Char stuffed the processed bear into one of the Billy's freezers. They washed up and headed outside, carrying a few steaks that they hoped Margie Rose would turn into a work of art. Char secreted a few pounds of flank steak that she'd eat later, raw as she preferred.

They collected their horses, thanked Billy for washing and grooming them, and then rode off. Once out of earshot, they both tried to talk at the same time.

Terry deferred, preferring to hear what Char had to say.

"I need to leave or he'll come back. Next time, he'll kill you on his way to me. Don't think your silver knife intimidated him," she cautioned. Terry shook his head. He hadn't thought that at all. His knife looked puny compared to the massive body of the alpha.

"Maybe it's time we took to the Wasteland, started looking for others. What will he do if you're not here?" Terry asked.

"Probably nothing. It's me he wants. He doesn't really care about humans." She looked at the ground as she talked, replaying the earlier encounter in her head.

"Look what he did to those two hunters. He has a taste for human flesh, and he'll be back alright, but will the pack come with him?" Terry wondered.

"The pack will only passively support him. No one is strong enough to challenge him alone. I need to leave, and it'll probably be best if you go with me, if you want to live," she suggested, reaching across the space between their horses to put a hand on Terry's arm.

Clyde yipped as the horses walked together, squeezing out from in between them. He ran ahead, turning into the brush when he caught sight of a rabbit. He started braying as he chased the terrified creature.

"So, what do we tell Margie Rose? For a woman who rarely leaves the house, she always knows everything that's going on, so we won't be able to keep your ex-husband a secret for very long…"

CHAPTER NINE

Marcus was furious. He shook with the anger that raged through his body. He needed to kill something, badly. "With me," he roared at no one in particular. So they followed as he changed into Werewolf form and ran into the woods, faster and higher until he smelled the bull elk. He raced after him, wanting the creature to run.

It did, as Marcus neared. It pounded the earth with its heavy hooves, leaping ravines and tearing through the brush with reckless abandon.

He followed it, pacing himself faster than the fleeing bull. He ran it down from behind, leaping onto its back and biting deep into the creature's neck, trying to drag it down so he could snap the spine or change his grip to the bull's throat.

The elk twisted as it fell and its neck broke, almost too easily. Marcus jumped aside deftly, staying clear of the horns when the elk hit the ground. He waited to make sure it was dead before ripping the flesh apart, feasting on the great beast.

He called the rest of the pack to him, and they each dug in.

❖ ❖ ❖

Margie Rose wasn't convinced by their story about the stranger, but they wouldn't tell her more. She let it go, because it cast a storm cloud over her home. They'd already finished their dinner, but Margie Rose added a freshly baked biscuit that she covered with a gracious helping of jam. Terry and Char looked forward to their dessert, but Clyde had different ideas.

He tripped Margie Rose and when the biscuits flew across the living room, he gobbled them one by one, until he was ushered outside, none too kindly, at the end of Margie Rose's broom. They wouldn't let her make any more, although she insisted. It had been a long day, so they packed it in.

Terry lay awake, his mind running a hundred miles an hour. A Werewolf invasion. Holy shit. Marcus was a mountain of flesh, and Terry didn't have a way to fight him.

The doorknob slowly turned and Char stepped through, closing the door quietly behind her. Wearing nothing but panties, she walked to the side of the bed and stood for there for a second. Terry slid over and she crawled in next to him. She curled into the crook of his arm, putting her head on his chest and listening to the beating of his heart. It sped up, then slowed back to its rhythmic pace.

"What's this, are you afraid of him?" Terry finally asked.

"You'd be a fool not to be afraid. You saw what he's capable of. But I'm not afraid for myself. My life was forfeit the second I walked away from him. I'm afraid that I won't be able to protect you," she whispered.

Terry was taken aback. He understood that he needed her protection when the fight came. Marcus would kill him and eat his heart. The thought twisted his stomach into a knot.

Terry threw the covers off as the heat in the bed increased dramatically. He'd already started to sweat. Lying next to a Werewolf was worse than having Clyde sleep on him. "Hey! It's cold in here," Char complained. He pulled the covers over her and caressed her hair as she drifted off. Clyde was howling outside, leaving Terry no choice.

He carefully tucked a pillow under Char's head and tiptoed from the room, downstairs, and to the front door. When he opened it, Clyde sprinted through. "Keep it down, Clyde!" Terry snagged a piece of cooked bear for the dog, but he couldn't be sure Clyde even tasted it as he gulped it down.

Terry tried climbing the stairs quietly, but Clyde was all toenails and sliding. When he opened the door, he saw the bed was empty, the covers neatly pulled up to the pillows. He sighed, happy in one way and sad in another, confused in both.

Clyde took two steps and leapt over the footboard and into the middle of the bed where he curled up. "No you don't, you flea-bitten mongrel!" Terry jumped on the bed beside Clyde, bouncing him into the air. When he landed, Terry expertly moved him to the side and wriggled under the covers.

The door opened and Char walked back in. She closed the door behind her and made her way to the bed, pointing for Terry to move over. He looked at Clyde who had rolled onto his side and was stretching out his long legs.

Terry held up his hands in surrender.

Char nodded then grabbed the mattress and pulled it up,

shaking the whole thing once. Clyde hit the floor first, followed closely by Terry. Char shook the mattress back into place and crawled in.

When Terry stood up, he thought turnabout was fair play. He grabbed the mattress, but without opening her eyes, Char waved a finger at him. "Don't even think about it, TH." Clyde leapt past him and that was all the incentive Terry needed. He scrambled under the covers, kicking and pushing Clyde until the dog resigned himself with sleeping at the foot of the bed.

"We need to figure out how to beat him. I can't do it alone, not yet anyway, and you can't stand up to him on your best day, with your best weapons at hand," she sighed.

"When I believe I can't beat him, then I will have already lost. There's always a way to win. I just need to find it," Terry whispered. "And I will find it, because we're not here to protect ourselves. We're here to protect everyone else, the engineer, the mechanic, even Billy and Felicity."

She nodded, rolled to her side, and was soon asleep. Clyde started to snore. And Terry laid there, the foot under Clyde was sweating and he thought he was getting a heat rash on his left side because of Char. The Marine Corps way was to embrace the pain, drive it to its apex, let it know that it couldn't defeat you.

He wrapped an arm around the Werewolf and pulled himself close, closed his eyes, and started to sweat. He finally surrendered and pushed himself away. He balanced himself on a sliver of the bed as far away as possible from the Werewolf and the dog.

The cool of his precarious position was a welcome respite and sleep embraced him.

When the morning came, Char sat up, stretched, and got out of bed.

"That was the best sleep I've had in long time, TH. You are a dynamo in the rack!" she teased. "Come on, Clyde. Let's see what the new day has to offer while we let Mr. Late Sleeper get his beauty rest. Heaven knows he needs it." Char opened the door to find Margie Rose shuffling past.

Margie Rose stopped, looked at the barely dressed young woman, then pulled her into a matronly hug. She peeked past her into the bedroom where the covers were thrown about and Terry lay with his arm over his head, looking at her with one eye open. She waggled her fingers at him. Terry closed his eye and wished for more sleep.

"Get some clothes on, young lady! I will make you the best breakfast you've ever had. I'm sure you need to get your energy back," Margie Rose said, giggling, followed by smacking her wooden spoon on the scantily clad Char's perfectly rounded butt. "Now get dressed!"

❖ ❖ ❖

"Get your lousy asses out of the rack!" Devlin yelled at the newcomers. It had been three days and all they'd done was every type of physical fitness activity that Mark, Devlin, Jim, and Ivan could think of.

The new recruits were breaking down. They couldn't seem to do anything right, were reactive all the time, and were late to everything.

Exactly like they were supposed to be. When Terry and Char arrived, the FDG formed in two ranks. The first had the original four members and the second rank had the newcomers. Terry wasn't pleased with that. He wasn't happy with himself for spending so much time away from his recruits. Even the old ones were new and needed to learn.

He waved them into a circle around him.

"Here's what's going on," Terry started, looking to Char then back to the group. "There's a new man, who's watching us right now from the mountains." Terry hesitated, not sure how much to share. He knew that he couldn't tell them the truth.

"It's Char's ex-husband and this man is bigger than any human being you've ever seen before." Terry hung his head. "That means Char is his target. Tactically, we can't have a battle here. Our job is to protect this town, and if, by our presence, we create a greater risk, then it follows that we need to move. Here's what we are going to do…"

Terry moved the small group to a dirt patch beside the barracks' yard. He drew New Boulder, Denver, south to New Mexico and east through the worst of the Wastelands to Kansas.

"It looks like it's not going to be cold enough to get a good snow, but it will be cool enough to travel east. So, we're going to take four of you north, find the South Platte River and follow it, see if there are any settlements, see if we can find people. If that doesn't bear fruit, we'll head south, cross the Wastelands until we find the Arkansas River, and then we'll follow it back to Pueblo, and look for the stash on our way back through Colorado Springs and home." He looked from face to face. Char stood behind the group, shaking her head and rolling her eyes.

The stash of arms and equipment was his white whale. Char was right. He couldn't let it go. He was building an army and needed to be the biggest and baddest. He couldn't do that with bows and arrows. He couldn't stand up to Werewolves or worse, the Forsaken, with just rifles. Terry needed C4. He needed flamethrowers and grenade launchers. He needed anything and everything the U.S. Military might have stashed at one time and never come back for.

Had he been active duty during the World's Worst Day Ever, he would have moved much of the armory to a secondary location, secure in its anonymity. He expected his brothers-in-arms would think the same way.

And then he hoped that those alternate locations hadn't been found.

Twenty years was a long time, but after the first one or so, the scavenging had drawn down. People settled in to just survive, hunting and gathering like humans had done centuries past. The advanced world tried to destroy everything it had built, but humanity had survived. Technology survived. The people just needed to clean it up and put it back into place.

Infrastructure. They needed factories, facilities to make microchips, raw materials to send to the factories. It was a monumental undertaking.

Terry gave himself one hundred years. As long as he didn't get his head cut off or maimed so badly that the nanocytes couldn't do their thing, he'd see his new world take shape.

To do that, he needed to eliminate the threats to peace.

Like Marcus.

Terry clenched his jaw and growled. They'd leave, train on the road, prepare themselves to fight a Werewolf, then they'd return.

The Force members looked at Terry uncomfortably as he'd turned silent and showed a wide range of emotions through his facial expressions.

It was time to turn the Force into a real military organization. He'd thrown out some ranks and such, but they never used the titles or embraced the concept of chain of command. As the Force grew, he needed that discipline and structure to be part of their very souls.

No time like the present.

"Okay, my pretties," he said in his best drill instructor voice. "Here's how it's going to be. If you don't like it, then you can spar with me. We'll decide the issue through hand-to-hand combat. Do you understand me?"

A hearty chorus of "yes, sir" greeted him in response as they jumped to their feet.

"You snot-gobbling, slack-jawed, jelly-bellied, tiny-dicked..." Char waved at him mid-sentence. He looked at her angrily as she pointed to one of the newcomers. Lacy leaned out so TH could see her.

"I'm a chick, sir," she said. He hesitated for half a heart-beat before continuing.

"...no-dicked pieces of gutter slime. You will refer to me as Colonel Walton or sir. My executive officer is Charumati. You will call her Major. I know, she was a private last week, but that was last week. I need her as my XO. James and Mark are my corporals and your squad leaders. Mark will be responsible for the security of New Boulder in our absence. You will have Jim, Ivan, Boris, David, Charlie, and Blackbeard to help you. See that they are armed at all times. You will need to provide twenty-four hour security for the mayor. That is your primary mission. Secondary is the security of the power plant and the greenhouses.

"James and his squad--Devlin, Lacy, and Geronimo--will accompany Char and me. Any questions?"

The men shifted uncomfortably. Terry stood and stabbed a finger into Mark's chest. "Out with it!"

He looked at the others before speaking. "I'm sorry, sir,

but I'd like to go too, probably all of us," he said weakly. Terry grabbed him by the shoulders and shook him, smiling at the corporal.

"There's a big nasty out there. He's coming after Char so we are taking her away from here. That doesn't mean he won't come back to New Boulder. I don't think he'll be as great a threat, but if he comes back, you will be fighting for your lives, the hardest fight you'll ever have. I can't leave the town unprotected. And you, Mark, are the best person to honcho that effort. You get good people to help, but you need to train them at the same time they're pulling guard duty. I know you haven't gotten that much training yourself, but of all the people here, you're the one who can pull it off," Terry said, never taking his hand from Mark's shoulder.

"Maybe you can stay here, and Char..." Terry cut him off.

"The major," Terry corrected.

"...the major can take the others out," Mark added hopefully.

"This is what I need. I want everyone to feel comfortable enough to speak their minds. There will be times when we can't have a conversation, and you'll know when those are. That time is not today, so we'll talk, make sure that we decide what's best for everyone." Terry looked at the map he'd drawn, thinking how to shape his argument on why he needed to be with Char that wouldn't look self-serving.

Char stepped beside Terry and looked at the group. "What the colonel seems hesitant to tell you is that I will have to fight my ex-husband myself. If I'm to win, I need to get better at hand-to-hand and that's why wherever I go, the colonel must go, too. I am in training from this moment forward with the singular goal of defeating, in unarmed combat, a man twice my bodyweight with longer reach and vastly greater strength. I need to become the deadliest fighter ever. And then I need to win that contest, protect all of you from hell incarnate."

"But you loved him once," Devlin stated, unsure of how the ex-husband thing worked.

"Maybe I was given no choice in the matter. There are places on this planet where women are little more than a man's property," she replied, giving everyone a small peek into what it was like to be her.

Terry clenched his fists in anger, furious at the injustice, but calmed as he knew that he would keep such things from his world and would prevent those under his influence from devolving.

Again.

Char continued, "We'll be going tomorrow, so horses. You four, get six horses, four that you'll ride, two to take as spares. I believe the Mongols invaded and conquered half the world by taking four horses for every warrior. We don't have that luxury and we aren't on a conquest, so two extras to pack gear should we find the colonel's white whale. Mark! Establish the guard rotation and put the men in place. We will inspect your setup this afternoon. Is that understood?" She clapped her hands and waved the Force away.

"Yes, sir," Mark replied, locking his body at the position of attention. The others mirrored his position for an instant before running off. Mark and James corralled their designated people and pulled them close for private conversations.

Terry looked sideways at Char. Where in the hell had that come from? In her previous life, had she served in the military? He didn't know that, or hardly anything else, about her. He needed to find out, get her to talk more while he talked less.

Char turned to him and asked, "What do you think, Mr. Colonel TH, sir?" She smiled as she tried to stifle a laugh.

It wasn't a game, but she played her role well. "I hope that man-mountain doesn't return before tomorrow," Terry told her. She stopped smiling and punched him in the stomach with a short jab. His gear protected him from most of it.

He rolled into the punch, grabbing her arm as he continued downward, pulling her off-balance. Terry dove forward and twisted, throwing Char to the ground as he let go, hit, rolled, and came back to his feet. The ten members of the Force watched, wide-eyed.

Char attacked, jumping into the air for a vicious roundhouse. Terry ducked it and dodged to the side, sweeping a leg past her. But he hadn't put enough into it and kicked her leg, not enough to take it out from under her. She leaned forward and punched him in the back as he continued past.

Terry stood and danced, shaking off the pain from Char's last punch. The nanocytes kicked into overdrive as his natural adrenaline surged, sharpening his senses and hardening his body. Char continued in the attack, feigning and striking, left, right, high, low. Terry blocked most of the blows, but some got through, and he started to tire.

Char went for the haymaker, choosing an axe-kick, a straight overhead kick bringing the heel down on the defender's head to drive the person to the ground.

But Terry wasn't that tired. When her leg went up, he lunged forward, trapping her leg against her body. He lifted her and drove her body back and down, into the ground. He dropped to a knee and punched her repeatedly in the abdomen. She tried to backflip out of Terry's hold, but he had her in place where she couldn't get her leg under her.

He called a halt, and she conceded. Char was faster and

stronger, but she'd lost the bout. Terry was breathing hard and sore from the pounding he'd taken. Char flexed her midsection, feeling the strain from TH's flurry of punches that ended it.

Terry turned to their impromptu audience, standing in amazement. "The man that could be coming is bigger and faster than either of us. Understand what you're up against. Don't be afraid, just be aware and know that if you ever go anywhere without your weapon, you will have no chance at all."

"What the fuck are you gawking at!" Char screamed. Half of the men jumped and the others cowered, but only for a moment before running away like rabbits.

"Shall we, TH?" Char asked, grabbing Terry's arm as they walked away. Clyde had been silent through it all. They wondered if he was okay. His head and tail hung as he walked. Terry stopped, kneeled, and looked at him. Bloodshot eyes, lids droopy.

"You're tired, aren't you, buddy? Me, too, Clyde, me too."

Char laughed as she left the commiserating, tired old men and headed toward the mayor's house. They needed to talk.

CHAPTER TEN

"We hunt, you worthless fucks," Marcus growled. The pack wasn't sure they could eat any more. Three elk in as many days, but Marcus's appetite seemed insatiable. The only thing that lightened his mood was tracking and killing the largest of the bull elk. He reveled in fighting those with a rack and trying to defend themselves. Marcus unleashed his full rage upon the unwitting creatures.

One more, then he'd take the whole pack into the human settlement and bring Char out of there one way or another; either she could walk out or they'd drag her carcass into the hills and dump it there.

Marcus walked away from the pack, expecting them to follow, which they reluctantly did, grumbling the whole way. He dumped his clothes in the crook of a tree branch and shape-changed.

The great, black Werewolf sniffed the air and reached out with his senses. There was something different coming from the mountains, something big and mean. Exactly what he wanted. He turned and angled away to stay downwind. He growled at the pack to remain behind and to keep quiet. Marcus slinked away, silent as the falling snow.

He felt the bear coming and got into position. A worthy adversary. The bear raised up on his back legs and looked around, sniffing excessively. Marcus ruffled his hair, felt that the wind had changed. The bear could smell him.

What matter?

With a roar, he raced through the trees, singularly focused on the grizzly that waited up ahead. Marcus sped past the last tree and in two bounds, leapt, jaws open as he angled his muzzle toward the creature's throat. The bear's paw swiped, faster than the eye could see, and Marcus was thrown away, maimed by the bear's claw, ribs exposed by the angry slash through the Werewolf's fur.

Marcus looked stupidly at the wound. The bear roared and dropped to all fours as it charged, turning the tables on the Werewolf. Marcus jumped straight in the air, turning to land on the grizzly's back, but the bear's jaws were faster and clamped on the Werewolf's back leg, crushing the bone just above the back paw. The bear shook its head and threw Marcus to the side.

He stood on three legs, suffering the real pain of a horrible wound along with the blow to his ego. The only time he feared for his life during a battle had been at the hands of a Forsaken, but that wasn't a battle to the death, only to teach him a lesson. Marcus's life had not been in jeopardy, but he hadn't known that at the time.

The bear circled, looking to press his advantage, then

throwing caution to the wind, he charged. Marcus's body was already healing itself. He'd eaten enough that his energy was at its peak.

The bear thought he was wounded and vulnerable. Marcus let the bear get close, then dodged backward as the grizzly slapped a paw at him. The Werewolf darted forward and planted his jaws on the grizzly's massive neck.

The bear tried to throw Marcus off, but couldn't reach him. The grizzly backed up and twisted his whole body around in a circle, lifting Marcus off the ground and swinging him wildly. But the Werewolf hung on, grinding his teeth in the flesh, trying to rip out the artery that fed the creature's brain. With another swing, Marcus was thrown off, carrying a mouthful of the bear's neck with him.

Blood spurted in a long arc, then again. The bear shook its head, trying to clear its fading vision. It sat back, then tipped to the side and fell over. Its eyes glazed, surprised that it lost a fight to a lone wolf.

Marcus staggered forward, his leg in agony and fire burning along his side. He howled to his victory, but it was weak, not his usual bellow. The pack slowly appeared and took positions around the bear. He wondered if they were going to rise up against him

But no, even in his weakened state, they were afraid of him.

He bit into the grizzly, tearing a hunk of meat from its chest. He chewed slowly, but ran out of steam. He leaned against the grizzly, feeling the warmth of its fur, closed his eyes and fell asleep.

❖ ❖ ❖

"What in the fuck do you mean you're leaving? Fuck no! FUCK NO!" Billy screamed almost hysterically.

"Language, Billy dear," Felicity cooed from the loveseat against the wall. His head whipped around, and he glared at her, almost feral.

Fear did that to people. Billy thought Marcus would return. And Terry couldn't convince him otherwise because he believed the Werewolf would be back.

"Billy Spires, Mayor of New Boulder," Terry started. "I'm leaving you with seven people and I've directed them to set up a twenty-four seven guard for you. They are to be armed at all times. With that kind of firepower, they'll be able to hold Marcus off." Terry had a hard time looking at Billy because he knew for a fact that his men and their rifles wouldn't deter Marcus.

Billy sat down heavily and slouched in his chair. He was adamantly opposed to his security chief leaving when such a threat was nearby.

Char spoke, "He's come for me, Billy. He doesn't care about you or anything you have. He only cares that he's lost his property. He wants what he considers to be his, and I can't have that, but I also can't have him tearing up this town to get to me. You need to trust me that he will know that I've left. He may follow us, will probably follow us, but we'll lead him far away from here. That's best for everyone, Billy." Char was leaned forward, elbows on the table, looking intensely at the mayor as if trying to sway him with the power of her mind.

Which Terry thought she could do. He didn't interfere, because she was right. New Boulder would not survive an attack by the pack.

❖ ❖ ❖

Mark considered for a second, "Twenty-four seven coverage. Twelve hour shifts. Nightwatch, you take the nights. We change after dawn and toward dusk. We'll have a second watch change at noon and midnight. Twelve on, twelve off until the colonel returns, with one pair changing out every six hours," Mark explained to the assembled group. He needed four people for his plan. He had seven at his disposal. He'd rotate people in and out and the three who weren't active would train in firearms, physical fitness, tactical movement, and everything he'd learned in the two months of study under Terry Henry Walton.

There was so much that he didn't know, but committed to learning. He'd started taking notes, using an old pencil and a notebook that he'd found when surveying homes for the newcomers.

"As the colonel said, none of us is as smart as all of us, so if you see something or think something, share it. Let's find what works best." Mark looked at those in his charge. He'd never been responsible for so many before. Once, he would have been drunk with power, but now, his goal was to not disappoint Terry. He gave his full attention to the mission.

The *mission*.

"The largest human being you'll ever see could come this way, and then what do we do?" Mark asked.

"Shoot him dead!" Boris suggested with a smile.

"Maybe, but that's not the first thing we do. What did the colonel teach us?" Mark asked, looking at Jim and Ivan.

Jim shrugged. "He beat the crap out of me three times before I finally figured it out."

Ivan pointed to his crooked nose and misshaped lip. "He smashed my face in."

Mark held his head, then threw up his hands in frustration.

"He gave us a chance. We fought him when he was willing to talk first. Had we discussed things, then we wouldn't have gotten our asses handed to us. Again and again. So we'll talk, but we have to be ready to fight. We'll have two people awake and on shift at any point in time. The first who sees this man or any new person sounds the alarm and then stops that person to talk…"

The seven of them practiced saying "stop, identify yourself and your purpose here!" Blackbeard was the most animated as he put himself into the role, imagining it was Sawyer Brown but with the roles reversed. Blackbeard was the one with the rifle, smaller, with power to kill at his fingertips.

"Corporal?" Blackbeard asked, and Mark acknowledged him. The others turned, wondering. "When do we get our guns?"

Guard duty was to start that night and only half his people were armed. "Which of you know about the AK-47?" Blackbeard was the only one who did not raise his hand. "We have a couple days to teach you all about your rifle and how to shoot, Blackie." The young man looked disappointed

"Nightwatch, you assume your shift after dinner. Go get some rack time. David, you start at midnight. Get yourself some sleep. The rest of us, we're going to build a guard shack where I'll sleep, so either I or Jim can be here all the time. That will give us three people to respond and we'll have Billy to back us up, too. He'll be watching from up there, just like he is now," Mark said, pointing at the second-story window where Billy stood, leaning against the frame and looking out at the group of men who were his security.

"Let's make them proud. We stand between the unknown and the new world, where people can live their lives without interference from people like I used to be. That world sucked.

I like this new place that Terry Henry, Char, I mean the colonel and major, and even Billy Spires are building. Can you imagine flipping a switch and having light and heat? We're going to get there. All we have to do is stand guard, so we will stand guard better than anyone has ever done before, because it is what we must do." Mark hesitated, then decided he'd lectured enough.

He stayed with Blackie while Ivan and David found themselves a place to get some sleep. The other three went in search of materials to build a guard shack, a small building where they could put a cot and clean their weapons after being out in the weather.

The young man looked at Mark with respect, eager and wanting to learn. Mark knew that he couldn't let the young man down. It would have been like failing his own children, and that was how he felt about all of the men in his squad. *Damn you, Terry Henry! I never wanted to be a dad, but here I am, me and my six kids.*

He finished his thought, *And I wouldn't have it any other way.*

"This is the AK-47. It is a magazine-fed automatic and semi-automatic weapon that fires a 7.62 by 39mm round…" he recited, pointing to the parts on the weapon as he talked.

❖ ❖ ❖

"It feels good to be back in uniform. Wearing street clothes, I felt like a partisan or something," Terry said casually as they walked toward Margie Rose's house. He looked at Char in her skin-tight jeans. "How can you wear those?"

"Well, TH. I wear them well," she replied, one eyebrow raised, purple eyes sparkling.

"It's going to be a really long ride. We'll be on those horses for weeks. And how are you going to be able to practice fighting while wearing them?"

"Loose jeans or tight jeans will make a difference in how I sit in the saddle?" she asked sarcastically. "You understand that when I fight Marcus for real, I'll be in my Were form?"

Terry pursed his lips. He hadn't considered that. "That changes things a bit. If you fight me as a Werewolf, can you keep yourself from killing me?"

"Why would I want to kill you?" Char was confused.

"I read books. In *Harry Potter*, the Werewolf wasn't in control," he countered, trying to keep it light while his mind worked on how to train a Werewolf in her natural state.

Char stared at him, "*Harry Potter*? You mean to tell me that everything you know about Werewolves, you learned from *Harry Potter*?"

"Not really. I've run across them before, but I don't really know anything. So you are you, regardless of form," Terry conceded. "Purple eyes and all."

"Exactly. Marcus is a great black Werewolf, huge jaws and unrivalled physical strength. I need to be faster, stay away from his mouth, get in behind him. I need to end the fight quickly." She looked into the distance as she imagined how the battle would play out. Marcus trying to dominate her through brute force.

But he was fast, too. She needed to be faster.

"We're going to have to tell the others," she said matter-of-factly.

"I think so, because you are going to have to get in shape, work out as a Werewolf, run, build muscle, turn on a dime. Which means that we need to feed you well, too," Terry said as his mind continued to work at the speed of light.

"I will hunt for us all. In Were form, I'm a pretty good hunter, but you are right. I will need to eat a lot."

They continued walking back toward Margie Rose's house in order to make sure the horses were ready for an early morning departure and that their bags were packed with everything they needed. They didn't have much in the way of material goods. Terry thought he'd be able to talk Margie Rose into making some hard rolls for the group, at least for the first day. After that, they'd be on their own.

"Silver," Terry said out loud, as his mind raced on a new tangent. "If I can braid some silver into my whip, what would that do?"

"Hurt like hell, leave a scar that would take a long time to heal. If you wrapped silver around his neck, he would have a hard time getting it off because it would hurt him to touch it," she answered. "But then he'd simply attack and kill you in a way that your nanocytes won't be able to save you."

"I figured that second part, but this would be a last resort kind of thing. I'm not going down without a fight. And if I'm fighting him with my bullwhip, then you've already lost. Maybe at that point he'll be hurt badly enough that I can finish him, then we can see if your nanocytes can come to the rescue," Terry suggested. "I can't lose my major. That wouldn't make me a very good colonel."

"Is that why?" She stopped to look at him, one hand on his arm. He turned to face her.

"Of course, what other reason could there possibly be?" He cradled her face in his hand before stroking the silver streak in her hair that trailed down one side of her face.

"Brown pelt, silver belly fur," she answered before he asked.

Clyde ran at them and jumped, hitting Terry in the chest.

He stumbled backward and fell. "What the hell, Clyde?" The dog dropped into play pose, tail wagging furiously. Char laughed and pointed an accusing finger at Terry.

"Saved by your dog. I'm starting to wonder about you, TH." Terry rolled to all fours and lunged at Clyde. The dog danced backward and ran off. Terry jumped to his feet and jogged after the big coonhound.

"Little boys. My pets are little boys!" she yelled after them.

CHAPTER ELEVEN

When Marcus woke, it was a full day after the bear attack. He'd been moved to the side, placed carefully among rocks protected by a stand of tightly-packed trees. He could smell the bear not far off as it was starting to rot. He crawled stiffly from the rocks. The wound along his side had healed, but there was an ugly scar. His back leg supported his weight, but it looked bulkier than his other leg. He wondered why it hadn't healed without leaving any trace of the original injury.

He'd think on that later.

His clothes were piled nearby, but he left them as he found the bear and ate, indifferent to the gamey taste. There was no trace of Were scent on the bear, but other predators had partaken, coyotes, birds, maybe even a wolverine. He couldn't tell for sure.

Marcus ate his fill of the greasy meat and then staggered

back to the rocks, where he curled up. He reached out with his senses, but couldn't find the others. They weren't close by and he hadn't seen a note. He changed into human form and dug through his clothes. Nothing.

They could have killed him, but they didn't. They could have left him for dead with the bear, where other predators would find him, but they didn't. They could have stayed to protect him, but they went somewhere.

My pack has gone to that town to get Char. They will return with her and then we will move on. With those thoughts comforting him, he went back to sleep.

He could not have been more wrong.

❖ ❖ ❖

That evening, Terry and Char rode the horses back to the mayor's house to inspect the guard. Char told TH to let her handle it, which he agreed to, but he wanted to know something first.

"Were you ever in the military?" he asked.

"Yes," she replied without elaborating.

"Well, out with it, branch of service, MOS, your military occupational specialty, what did you do?"

"Columbia, Naval ROTC, class of 1965. Women didn't serve on ships back then, so I was admin ashore. That sucked, so four and done."

"Ivy League," Terry said. She rolled her eyes and shook her head. "I'm thinking your real education came later, the real world education that made you who you are."

"Studying hard will not turn you into a Werewolf, Terry dear," she drawled, mimicking Felicity. TH smiled.

He wanted insight into the Werewolf who would protect

New Boulder with her life, just as he would. And that was why they were leaving, because it was best for everyone. If only they could get Marcus to follow, lead the pack as far away from the civilians as they could.

"How do we get the pack to follow us?" Terry asked.

❖ ❖ ❖

Billy Spires looked at the dog's breakfast being erected in his front yard. "What the hell is that?" Billy asked, then pulled the window open, shivering when the cool breeze hit him.

"Fuck no!" he yelled at the men below. "Nobody move, I'm coming down there!"

Mark looked at the others with trepidation. What if Billy's orders contradicted the colonel's? He didn't have long to wait as the mayor stormed out the front door.

"What the fuck is this monstrosity?" Billy asked.

"The guard shack?" Mark said, making it a question, just in case. "Shelter from the weather while a place for a third person to sleep, so we always have three people on hand."

"Why don't you just use the shed out back?" Billy replied, pointing toward the sidewalk that led to the back of the house. Mark held his hands up. He hadn't thought to ask.

Billy waved them to follow him as he led the group to the back of his house. A shed was there, unlocked. There was very little in it. Once they moved the freezer out, there would be enough room for a cot, two chairs, and a small table where they could clean their weapons. The only drawback was they couldn't see the front of the house from the shed.

It was never Mark's intent to stand guard duty from within the shack, so his people would be exposed to the weather a little more than planned. They'd deal with it.

"We have a triangle of steel that we'll ring if anyone approaches. That's our alarm, Billy. When you hear that, you'll know someone is coming, and you'll also know that there will be three of us with rifles, out here, between your house and him." Mark stood tall, looking confident.

He was a far different man from the one that Billy had used to bully the townspeople. John was that way naturally so he flourished in the role that Billy had put him into. John had bullied these men, as well. Mark stood there a new man, with a selfless purpose. The others, too. They were well armed and ready to do battle, even though they were ill-prepared to fight a man like Marcus.

Billy held out his hand and Mark shook it.

"Thanks, Mark, to all of you. Follow whatever orders Terry Henry gave you and for fuck's sake, tear down that bullshit in my front yard before Felicity sees it and rips me a new asshole," Billy quipped. The members of the Force chuckled until Mark gave them the Mark One hairy eyeball and they ran out front to tear down their attempt at building a guard shack.

"I trust you, but I hope to hell that big bastard doesn't come back here. If he does, there will only be one thing to do and that's fill him with holes. Lots and lots of holes…"

❖ ❖ ❖

Terry and Char saw the flurry of activity in Billy's front yard as they approached. Clyde started barking and ran into the middle of those he considered litter-mates since they all answered to his alpha and her beta.

Chaos ensued until they chased Clyde away. Mark walked from behind the mayor's house, kneeled down, and ruffled the dog's ears to keep him distracted while the men finished their work.

Char held her hands out, palms up in the universal WTF gesture. Mark jogged over, waving. "Don't look at that. It's nothing. Just cleaning up a little miscue. We've established the guard shack out back and the rotation. Ivan and David are sleeping as they have the first two shifts. Here, let me walk you through what we have in mind," Mark started.

Terry stopped him. "Here's a lesson I learned a long time ago. It's called Napoleon's corporal. In the old days, Napoleon conquered nearly all of Europe. One of his leadership tools was to tell his plan to a corporal. If the corporal could repeat it back to him, then the plan was simple enough to be followed by everyone involved. So, Blackbeard will brief the plan once you remove whatever it is you've got going on here," Terry told them, squinting, unable to make heads or tails out of why this mass of varying building materials was in the front yard.

The men loaded up and carried everything to a nearby burn pile. They returned and formed up into their squad, with Mark at the front and Blackie in the back. The men were armed with AK-47 rifles and magazines inserted. TH nodded for Char to lead the way.

Columbia Naval ROTC. Who would have thought that? No wonder she has a soft spot for the Marines, Terry thought, letting his ego out of its dark place for a short visit. Then he remembered why he went into the Wastelands, how his wife and son had been killed.

How Terry Henry Walton had not been able to save his own family.

He stuffed his ego back into its closet and slammed the door. His men weren't ready to do what he asked of them, but they were all he had. He needed Marcus to follow Char, and that was the only way the infantile Force de Guerre had a fighting chance.

Terry and Char dismounted, stood in front of Mark, saluted sharply, and started their inspection. The men didn't have uniforms, so they inspected the one thing that was available. The weapons.

Char looked over the AK-47 that Mark held in front of him. He turned it one way then the other for her. She nodded and moved to the next in line. Jim presented his rifle and Char ripped it out of his hand. She snarled. "Look at this!"

Jim was confused.

"Your selector switch is set for automatic fire!" she screamed at him. His eyes grew wide. "Am I going to find a round in the chamber, Private? AM I?"

Jim nodded weakly. Char pulled on the magazine release lever in front of the trigger housing and removed the magazine. She grasped the lever aside the bolt and yanked it to the rear, sending a live round out the ejection port and to the ground some feet way. She jammed the rifle so hard into Jim's chest, it sent the big man staggering backward.

"Put your weapons on safe and get your finger off the trigger!" she growled at them.

Terry wondered how much time she spent with the Marines. Maybe too much as she seemed a natural in her role, but that was an awful long time ago. Nothing to be jealous of, and why would he feel jealous in any case? He shook his head to clear his mind, getting angry with himself.

If his men were not up to speed then he didn't train them well enough. It was his responsibility. *I need more time*, he argued within his own mind. *But you don't get any more time. Tomorrow, you run, leaving a trail that a child could follow in hopes that a Werewolf will come after you. Not your best plan, TH, but there wasn't anything better out there, so off you go, dickweed.*

Terry was harder on himself than anyone else could ever be. He didn't give others that kind of control over his life. He answered to himself alone.

Char continued the inspection while Terry fought his internal battle. When he came back to the present, he found that Char had moved two people down the row. He whispered a few kind words to Jim and then to Boris as he caught up with her.

She didn't have to wonder what he was thinking about. He was putting these men in harm's way and they were woefully underprepared. She was chewing on them enough to give them weeks of material to think about. When she finished with Blackbeard, whose weapon was completely unloaded, she had to ask. "No ammo, Private?"

"I was just given my weapon this afternoon, Major. The corporal said I have a few more lessons before I'd get ammunition. I don't stand watch for four more days. I'll be ready, ma'am!" he proclaimed.

"Now that is the smartest thing I've heard today!" she bellowed. A glint from the upstairs window showed Billy and Felicity both watching with great interest. Felicity waved to Terry, who didn't acknowledge her.

"Weapons discipline is important in all situations. Blackbeard!" she called, even though he was standing in front of her. "Brief me on the guard plan."

"Can I show you?" he asked. She nodded tersely.

He walked to the far corner and started his long explanation as to why that spot was the first point while the two men of the guard worked their post. One looking one way and one looking the other at all times, both looking in the direction that Marcus had last come from, the road that led to the mountains.

Blackie also beat on the metal triangle with a small bar, making it ring. Each guard would carry one at all times, ready to sound the alarm.

He walked them through the routine and then showed them the guard shack behind the mayor's home. Char injected ideas here and there, but overall, she was satisfied with the plan and the squad's understanding of it. She formed them up one last time. Clyde ran wild through the group and discipline failed as he encouraged them one by one to pet him.

Char turned to Terry. "You need to get your privates under control?" He started to laugh, but caught himself, unsure whether she was joking or not. She didn't look like she was joking, but that shit was funny, especially while Clyde continued to wreak havoc.

"Clyde! Come here, boy," Terry called, kneeling to draw the dog his way. Char resumed.

"Well done, Private Blackbeard," she intoned, working not to roll her eyes at saying the name. "I like your plan. I like your engagement. I can't tell you how important it is to always be on alert, day or night. They could come at any time."

"They?" Mark asked.

"I meant he, he could come at any time, but who knows how many others are up there. Be ready for anything," she replied, trying to cover her mistake. The men looked confused.

Terry stepped in. "We will leave a trail for him to follow. If he shows up, you are to tell him where we've gone. It is best if he follows us. We're going north, then east along the South Platte River. There will be road signs and we'll leave signs, too. Your mission is to get him out of this town. I think you will find that despite his size, he will be an exceptionally difficult target to shoot at. If you fire, you must be prepared to die, so I prefer that you get him to follow us. Talk to him first. He'll know that Char has gone. Just tell him the truth. Any questions?"

No one had anything to say, even though Mark was curious as to why they wouldn't be able to hit this mystery man.

❖ ❖ ❖

When Marcus awoke, it was dark and he felt that most of his strength had returned. He returned to the bear for another meal, then settled in to wait, wondering when the pack would return with his mate. He'd give them until morning, then he'd go into town himself.

❖ ❖ ❖

James had gone through the packs three times already. There wasn't much, but Mrs. Grimes was a superhero in making sure they had the little that they did. Enough food for a couple days, if they rationed themselves.

He looked at the others, Devlin, Lacy, and Geronimo, an odd mix of people. James didn't understand why he was picked over Mark, or Devlin instead of Jim. One was older and smarter and the other was stronger than all of James's people combined.

They'd be on the road for a while. James hoped that he could pick the colonel's brain, learn how he thought, get smarter at the things that Terry Henry Walton valued.

They had time to kill, so James decided he needed to get to know his people better.

"Devlin, tell us about yourself. Why are you here?"

"I grew up here, my whole life spent foraging in the woods, farming, and doing odd jobs. I don't know, but Mark and John thought I could be useful, so they snagged me and Jim. Then there I was, one of the lawmakers. Our job was to intimidate people so they'd do as Billy told them. That was it. I hadn't been doing that long before Terry Henry showed up. He killed John, right there in the dining room, and then he gave us a choice. Reform or join John. That was a pretty easy decision," Devlin said, not looking at the others, feeling the shame of what he'd been before.

"What you were before doesn't matter, Devlin. That was a stupid question on my part. Lacy, tell me what you like about the FDG. Why did you join?"

"Because I believe in people. I grew up here, too and saw the recent change in everyone, especially Billy Spires. If Billy could change like that, then there's hope for us all. I want to be a part of making this world a better place. I believe in Terry Henry Walton and his vision for a new civilization. The people from Brownsville are the first of many to join us. I feel it in my bones!" Lacy offered with a smile.

She was young and wore her brown hair cropped tightly around her ears. She was short, stocky, and well-muscled. Like the other residents of New Boulder, she didn't have any fat on her body, but she wasn't starving. She had limited experience with horses, but she had grown up working in the power plant as a helper to the mechanic. She was born after the fall, and the mechanic looked after her once her parents passed. It was the least he could do for his niece.

James nodded and knew he'd talk with her later about the power plant. He was fascinated by it and wanted to know how the plant generated electricity.

"Tell us why you're here, Geronimo." James pointed to the small man.

"I finally have a chance to be somebody," Geronimo said in a small voice.

"What do you mean by that?" James pushed.

"You knew me, recognized that I existed back in Brownsville, but no one else did. I was just a lackey, a nobody. I lived in the stables with the horses. They are my only friends." He looked at the ground. James leaned over and put a hand on his shoulder.

"Not any more, Geronimo. I'll call you Gerry, because that's what friends do, give each other nicknames. You can call me Corporal!" He stood and clapped his hands. "Gerry! Why don't you select our six horses from the eight we have on hand and teach us a little about them? You are the expert, from what I understand."

Gerry beamed with pride and led the group to the horses where his love for them was obvious. He gently stroked each and they followed him around like puppies.

The four members of the FDG groomed the horses, made sure they were fed, then went to bed early, because they needed to be ready for when the colonel and the major arrived.

CHAPTER TWELVE

Terry and Char ate in silence while Margie Rose watched them.

"What's wrong with you two? Did you get into a fight?" she asked. They both perked up instantly, in full denial.

"Come on, Margie Rose, you don't think I'd rather be in a warm bed right here? We're both bummed because we have to lead a bad man into the Wastelands, as far from here as possible." Terry wiggled his eyebrows at the older woman, along with showing his most winning smile.

Clyde howled from somewhere outside. His attack on the biscuits had gotten him banned from the house during meal time.

"TH and I are good, don't you worry about that, Margie Rose. I mean really good," she said suggestively. Margie Rose blushed and Char giggled.

"By the way, I have a huge favor to ask," Terry started, his tone serious. "I've seen you wearing a silver necklace. Can I have that please?" He didn't tell her what it was for as she would probably object.

"Wait right here, you two!" she beamed. Char looked at her plate and shook her head, then started to clean off the table. Terry joined her, checking on the pot to make sure they had hot water to do the dishes.

Margie Rose returned with two necklaces, both tarnished just enough to show they were made of silver. She handed them both over. He looked at them appreciatively. The old woman put her hands in the small of his back and propelled him toward Char.

He decided to play along. He held the necklace up to put it over Char's head, but her eyes shot wide and she shook her head vigorously.

"Later, Margie Rose, when the time is right." He had wondered if just touching silver was enough to cause a Werewolf pain. Judging by Char's reaction, he would have hurt her had he put the necklace on, even gently so.

He pocketed the necklaces and gave Margie Rose a big hug and kiss on her forehead, before settling her on the couch, letting Clyde in, and returning to the kitchen to help Char with the dishes.

When they were done, they retired to Terry's room, where Margie Rose had already moved Char's meager belongings. By the light of a tallow candle, Terry uncoiled his bullwhip and carefully threaded the necklaces within the internal leather windings, closest to the tip where the bullwhip's speed was the greatest. Using a needle and thread, he put a stitch through the dainty links of the chain and into the black leather of the whip.

He wouldn't be able to test it until morning, when he had daylight to see if it would hold together. He wanted one extra weapon against Marcus.

He blew out the candle, stripped to his shorts, and wrestled with Clyde to get a spot in the bed. Char removed all her clothing and in the early darkness, changed into her Werewolf form. Clyde started barking until Terry could grab him and calm him down. Char put her front paws on the bed and sniffed both TH and Clyde.

Clyde bared his fangs and growled. Char returned the gesture and then snapped at his face. He yipped and crouched, starting to shake in fear. Terry let go and Clyde jumped down, crawling halfway under the bed.

TH stroked her head, scratching behind her ears. She leaned into his hand while her purple eyes, now three times their human size, looked at him. She bared her fangs and chuckled, at least he thought she was chuckling. He leaned down to see the light color on her chest.

"Silver belly fur," he said to himself, feeling how soft it was. He moved to the side of the bed, running his hands down her sides. As a she-wolf, she was big, taller than Terry Henry, with a broad chest and long muzzle. Her tail had long hair that swished through the air as she wagged it. He walked behind her and ran his fingers through her tail hair. "You have a tail."

She changed back into human form and glared at him for an instant before she climbed into bed and pulled the covers over herself.

"That's what you have to work with," she whispered. "That's what will fight Marcus."

"That was magnificent," Terry whispered back. "You have a tail."

"Of course I have a tail! I'm a fucking Werewolf," she replied, then smiled. "You're like twelve years old! How old are you, really?"

"Sixty-three," Terry answered softly. She looked at him, frowning, purple eyes twinkling in the darkness.

"I've always liked younger men," she said, then ended the banter and turned serious. "But none of that matters, TH, if we can't stop him."

"We'll see what tomorrow brings," he said as he rested his head on her bare chest. Her heart pounded a staccato into his ear. He lasted all of twenty seconds before his head started to sweat. He rolled to his side of the bed, throwing the covers off so he could cool off, wondering if he'd ever get used to the heat she projected.

Sleeping in the same bed with his wife had taken some getting used to, but he had liked it. It had been comforting to know that she was there, and it was just as comforting to have Char nearby, although for different reasons.

He had lost so much of himself when he hid in the mountains and wandered the Wastelands. He had condemned the old Terry Henry a million times over for his failures, for his inability to protect the ones he loved. Despite his outward appearance and drive, everything he did was for other people.

His bill was steep, and he didn't know if he'd ever be able to pay it off. Until then, there was nothing he could want for himself, not even a beautiful Werewolf who kept him warm at night.

That was the story he told himself anyway.

❖ ❖ ❖

The morning came early. Terry found himself underneath Clyde, who had finally decided to come out from under the bed. Char had an arm across his chest and he could swear he saw the skin starting to bubble.

It wasn't bubbling, but it was red, and worse, it itched. "Everybody off!" TH bellowed into the false dawn. Clyde jumped up, missed the edge of the bed, and splattered on the floor. Char didn't move except to open her eyes and glare at him. He quickly got out of bed to avoid getting punched, dressed in his uniform, and then lit the candle.

When he turned, Char was already dressed. He hadn't heard a sound, but he was growing more accustomed to that. He let Clyde out and the dog ran downstairs, where Margie Rose started yelling at the beast, then yips where he was chased outside with the assistance of her broom or wooden spoon. TH and Char walked downstairs together and Margie Rose beamed at them both.

She really wanted grandchildren. Terry wasn't going to be the one to break her heart, so he took Char's hand and smiled pleasantly, exercising extreme self-discipline to keep from scratching his chest.

They thought they would leave before Margie Rose got up, but they both hugged her for the welcome surprise, though they had little time. They wolfed their breakfasts down, then hugged the old woman once more before bolting out the door, saddling the horses, and yelling for Clyde.

They rode quickly to the barracks in the cool of the dawn. When they arrived, there was no delay. James and the others were already in the saddle and waiting. Terry turned toward the mayor's house to check in one last time before heading out of town.

They rode toward the mayor's house and were

appropriately challenged as they approached. "Halt, who goes there?" Even though Ivan could see who it was. Terry held up a hand for everyone to stop. Lacy was inexperienced with riding a horse and it took James grabbing the reins to stop the animal.

"Colonel Walton and his people," Terry replied. Ivan approached and shook Terry's hand and then Char's.

"Nothing to report, Colonel," Ivan said. David and Boris joined them, as did Mark. It was close to the changeover and although Ivan looked tired, he'd heard the group approach and had done the right thing.

"We're heading out. Remember what I told you and send him after us. Do not try to engage unless you're attacked first, then hit him with everything you have and keep pouring it on, even after you think he's dead. Do you understand me?" They nodded, then saluted. It made Terry cringe to see it, but he'd only spent ten minutes teaching them.

It wasn't up to his Marine Corps standard.

Terry collected himself and returned their salutes. "Carry out the plan of the day, Corporal," he ordered as he turned his horse's nose north, toward the power plant and beyond.

Terry kept his horse to a walk as he didn't want the sound of its hooves to wake anyone up before the work day started.

"Anything, Char?" Terry asked, wondering if Marcus was close enough for her to sense. She shook her head, looking relieved.

Once they passed the power plant, he urged his horse into a trot. Terry and Char rode up front, each staying close to the ditch on their side of the road, keeping the pavement between them. James and Lacy rode side by side as she couldn't control her horse yet. He trained her as they rode.

Geronimo and Devlin rode in the back, staying wide

apart like Terry and Char.

It became obvious quickly that Gerry was the best horse-man of the bunch. He seemed one with his horse while the others barely managed to keep their mounts going in the desired direction. None of the horses seemed comfortable around Char and the others didn't know why.

When they stopped at the end of their first long day, Terry would swear the group to secrecy, then tell them. He expected that their blind trust in him would help them internalize the news. He didn't know what he'd do if someone flipped out and ran.

He hoped they wouldn't, but he also knew that hope was a lousy plan. He needed a backup.

❖ ❖ ❖

Marcus stretched his Werewolf body as the first light broke through the trees. He changed into human form and got dressed for his walk back into town.

Marcus had grown angry overnight because he couldn't sense the others. He started to entertain the idea that the pack had abandoned him. His rage grew. It started with the humans. He never considered that his own actions drove the pack away.

"Don't you ungrateful fucks have enough to eat? Have an alpha who protects you? You better hope that I don't find you. I will fucking kill you all!" he yelled into the trees and the emptiness of his mountain. He stormed through the woods, through the new snow, heading downhill, always downhill.

New Boulder awaited him. He had business there that he would finish one way or another.

It was late morning by the time he made it to the rocky

outcropping that overlooked the town. A small plume of steam rose from the power plant. He couldn't see anything powered by the electricity, but expected that at night, the town would be lit up, almost like the old days. He missed those times.

Life was easier now, but harder in a different way.

The distractions and diversions of civilization made life worth living. Maybe that was what the others wanted. *They should have killed me*, he thought, *then they could have simply wandered into town and made themselves at home, play homemaker like it seems Char has done.*

And with that human, too. Marcus smelled the man's scent on her. He didn't like to lose. First his mate, then the pack. Marcus scowled as he leapt over the rock and jogged downhill.

Marcus's mind raced into a deep, dark hole where he was left alone to fight the entire world by himself.

"Challenge accepted, world, and fuck you!" he growled, picking up speed as he continued downward.

CHAPTER THIRTEEN

Felicity strolled outside with fresh baked bread, a generous helping of jam spread across the rough cut slices. Billy watched briefly from inside, drinking the concoction that replaced coffee. He couldn't remember what coffee tasted like. It had been too long and he hadn't drunk that much before the fall.

Felicity had made a pitcher of the stuff and Billy's job was to give the men drinks. He remembered when people brought him drinks. He wasn't too keen on serving coffee.

He shrugged into his coat and followed her out once she'd reached Mark and handed out the first couple slices. She had looked back to see if he was coming. He decided that he couldn't avoid it any longer.

When he reached Felicity, Mark and the man named Boris had their hands full. They kept one hand on their rifles, finger riding on the outside of the trigger guard and thumb resting on the selector lever. The other hand held their bread.

"I'll put this in the guard shack, stop by for a drink as you make your rounds," he offered and bolted without looking at Felicity. He decided to choose his battles wisely when standing up to her, but damn, when she was in a good mood, his life was incredible!

He'd been working on the side with the mechanic on a car that they both thought could be brought back from the dead, a 1930s roadster that had been locked away in a garage, but the engine was newer with a big carburetor that could burn a rougher fuel, a blend of alcohol and filtered ancient gasoline.

That was the hope, but their extra pair of hands, the young woman called Lacy, had joined the Force and already left New Boulder with Terry Henry. Billy would have to pick up his game and get up earlier in order to work on the car. Felicity usually slept in. She might not even know he was out of the house.

Billy put the pitcher in the guard shack. It would cool off quickly in the fall weather. He looked around and saw a towel, which he used to wrap around the pitcher as insulation. It could have been a rag. He couldn't tell anymore. It had been too long since there'd been any new towels, material, or anything.

He wanted a civilized society back, something he never thought he'd say. Terry was right. Civilization was better.

Now was the time for the real work in bringing humanity back to civilization.

When the alarm sounded, Billy was dicking around trying to keep a pitcher of coffee hot. He bolted from the shed and through the back door of his house, picked up his rifle where he'd leaned it by the front door, and continued outside.

Marcus was strolling up the road, head held high, lips

curled in an angry sneer.

Mark and Boris aimed their rifles at the man. Felicity stood frozen behind them.

"Felicity! Get in the house," Billy yelled, but she remained where she was. Billy ran outside. Mark started walking to the left while Boris went right. David ran from the far end of the route they'd mapped out.

Billy stepped in front of Felicity and aimed at the intruder.

"Halt!" Mark yelled. Marcus ignored him.

"She's not here and you know that. She went north, following the main road to where it crosses the South Platte River. Then they were going to take the river east, through the Wastelands. They are going to look for more survivors," Mark said.

Billy was shocked at what Mark was sharing.

Marcus stopped and looked at them. He sniffed the air and walked in a circle, not unlike a dog searching for a scent. Marcus looked north and started walking that way.

Mark held up a clenched fist. The men stayed steady as Marcus walked uncomfortably close to them on his way north. The members of the Force watched in awe as the massive man strutted past. Felicity shivered as she stayed behind Billy, keeping one hand on his shoulder to let him know that she was there.

Billy Spires let out the breath he'd been holding. His head pounded from the effort, and he blinked to clear his vision.

"Mark, maybe you can explain to me what that was all about?" Billy said more calmly than he felt.

"Yes, sir," Mark started as he approached the mayor, never taking his eyes from the man walking away. "The colonel insisted we tell Marcus exactly that. He said even with our rifles, we wouldn't be able to kill him, so not to try.

The colonel wanted to lead him away from town, fight him out there in the Wastelands."

That made sense to Billy. From what he knew of the man, Terry Henry would never put his people at risk if there was a different way. Once again, Terry did exactly what he said he was going to do. "Carry on," Billy said, mimicking what he'd heard from Terry.

The colonel.

It didn't mean anything to Billy, but it did to his security chief and Billy was learning to trust the man. It wasn't coming easy to him as he'd always counted on number one for his own security, but a growing town told him that he had to do things differently now, build infrastructure and establish stability of purpose while Terry provided the physical security. Together they created emotional security for the people to grow as a society.

"I'll be damned," Billy blurted.

"Not yet, Billy dear," Felicity replied, taking his arm as he slung his rifle over his shoulder.

"Don't forget, Mark, there's coffee for you and the boys in your shack," the mayor told the corporal as he and Felicity returned to the house.

❖ ❖ ❖

The horses had run freely up the road, through the ruins of what had been a robust series of suburbs, then to the northeast toward the abandoned town of Longmont. It then continued east where they ran into the trickle of water that formed the South Platte River. They'd marked their trail as they turned, using charcoal on the road.

But they moved quickly too, trying to keep the distance

up. Char suggested that at fifty miles a day, he could keep up without catching them. They could slow down when they hit Nebraska, but until then, they needed to keep up the pace.

They traveled with one break the first day. After midday, they stopped and Terry told James to establish a perimeter and maintain a watch focused on the way they'd just come. Terry and Char disappeared into the ruins of a small town.

Once safely on the other side, Terry watched Char undress, feeling like a voyeur as she did so. Once naked, she changed instantly into her Werewolf form, stretching very much like a big dog would. Terry pointed out a circuit for her to run a few laps while he setup up an obstacle course. She bolted away, throwing rocks and kicking up dirt as her paws and powerful legs drove her forward. Terry set up some obstacles that would force quick turns. Char made the first lap of what Terry thought should have been a half-mile in less than a minute, she churned through the tight turn at the end and raced off afresh.

He roughed in a few arrows to help guide her through the twists, at least on the first pass. She returned shortly and Terry waved her out for one more lap. Her tongue lolled out of her mouth as she pounded through the corner and away.

When she returned, he pointed out the marks on the ground and through the wreckage. She hit the first corner and jumped sharply left, then vaulted over a rusted truck, hit a wall and kicked off, landing in an open area, before running through a small maze, ending by working her way underneath overhanging debris.

"Again!" Terry shouted and she headed through it a second time. Terry cracked his bullwhip over her head when she was close enough. Then on the third pass, he threw chunks of wood on either side of her head. She caught the first three and missed the next two. She went through it again and caught four of the five.

Terry was throwing the wood blocks almost as hard as he could. No sense training to a low standard. After the last pass, he held out his arms and called a halt to the day's training. She panted heavily, head hanging low.

He scratched her behind her ears and stroked her neck. She stood on her back legs, putting her front paws over his shoulders. He hugged her to him and rubbed her sides as he did so. Then he found himself embracing a naked woman, finding his hand on her bare butt. He let go and tried to pull away, but she grabbed his head and planted her lips on his.

The heat, like fire, burned him without burning, like a hot sauce that one was used to. Terry lost himself for a moment and then pushed her away, looking at her in surprise.

"I'm not sure about this," he said, sounding very unlike the Marine Corps colonel he was trying to be. "Integrity and honor above all."

"What's any of that have to do with us?" she asked. "I can smell your pheromones. You can't hide that from me."

"The people I loved ended up dead. I don't know if I can love anyone again. Dammit, Char! We make a good team, and I don't want to lose you. Go on now, get dressed. I'm sure the others are waiting impatiently," he said, looking away.

Char took two steps with her shoulders slumped. When she turned back, she saw Terry watching her, eyes glistening. She straightened as he blinked rapidly. She closed her eyes and breathed deeply, smiling at the pheromones that poured from Colonel Terry Henry Walton.

"Someday," she whispered as he beat a hasty retreat to where they left the horses and the others. Then she stopped when she smelled something else.

❖ ❖ ❖

Marcus was running out of gas. He had been jogging for miles, following the charcoal marks on the roadway to keep going in the direction the others had gone. He'd sniff the ground on occasion to make sure the horses had come this way. He caught his mate's scent on the air, in areas where the wind hadn't touched it. But she was far ahead.

He kept going, maintaining his anger, but he was burning out. The healing process from the bear's injuries was taking more out of him than he wanted. He still had a ways to go. He finally stopped, because he needed to eat, which meant that he had to have enough energy to hunt, which he didn't.

Marcus found shelter in a small brick building. He curled up to sleep. He'd hunt after a nap and then he'd follow them, wherever they were going. He'd catch them and kill the humans, one by one, as Char watched. Then he'd have her, too. No one stood up to him like that.

No one. Not *ever*.

❖ ❖ ❖

Billy Spires walked through the power plant looking for the mechanic, but found the engineer first.

"Billy!" the man called out, always happy to see his benefactor. The mayor had treated both the engineer and the mechanic right from day one after the WWDE. "What brings you in today?"

"Just stopping by with a question. How many people are too many here in New Boulder?"

"We're not anywhere near that, Billy. This power plant? If we can improve the step-down transformers and distribution lines, we should be able to power a city ten times what we have now, as long as we use electrical heat sparingly or air conditioning in the summer. Those pull too large a load. Lights, cooking, and refrigeration shouldn't be a problem for a city of a thousand people," the man said, unsure if that was what Billy was looking for.

Billy studied the overhead piping of the small facility. Steam rose in odd places. Some pipes dripped water and other chemicals to the floor. The place looked like it was held together by spit and bailing wire.

"We need this place, engineer. Not going to fall apart or anything, is it?" Billy asked skeptically.

"It could use a little work, but we just lost one of our hands. Lacy joined your security people. What do they call it?" The engineer curled a lip when he asked the question.

"Force de Guerre, the FDG. I guess it means War Force or something like that. I don't speak Greek." Billy shrugged. "When they return, we'll make sure we get Lacy back in here, and some more help for you, too. As the greenhouses wind down for the season, will you be able to use some of those people?"

The man scratched his neck before answering, "Possibly. We need people who already have some mechanical skill. We can teach the others basics, but that takes time and takes us away from the main job of keeping the system dialed in, which reminds me, I need to get back to the control room." The engineer excused himself and hurried off.

Billy watched him go and continued his walk through the plant. He didn't understand any of the systems, only that the engineer and the mechanic had brought it back to life after the fall. Billy had given them the freedom to accomplish that.

Because he was a benevolent dictator. As Terry Henry

had told him, the world needed Billy Spires and Billy needed them, too.

Billy couldn't find the mechanic. He decided to leave and go work on the car until he could ask a question about the alternator. They'd taken it off and Billy had cleaned it up, but had no idea how or even if it worked.

The mechanic had taken the belts to the plant and carefully laid them in an area that was warm and filled with steam. He hoped that would rejuvenate the rubber so the belt would work as intended, turning the various shafts within the engine.

When Billy opened the door to the garage, he found the mechanic installing the alternator. "Billy! You did a great job on this. It looks to be generating electricity as it's supposed to. The battery is at the plant. We've tweaked up the acids inside and it looks to be holding a charge. You know what? I think this bitch is going to roll!"

The mechanic's grin was infectious. Billy rolled up his sleeves and prepared to dive in. Together they had kept at it, cleaning, scraping, grinding, and sanding as they rebuilt the engine, one step at a time. The mechanic loved the work, but he was getting older, already a good twenty years older than Billy. His hair had long since turned gray and his hands were gnarled from the hard work they'd done over a lifetime.

"Isn't it about time that you taught someone else, someone younger, mechanic?" Billy asked.

"Fuck you and the horse you rode in on," the man snapped back.

"I'm just thinking that you're getting older and look at everything you've learned in your life. You don't want to waste that!" Billy explained.

"I know exactly what you mean. When I die, poor Billy

Spires and his woman are going to be left out in the cold. Like I said, fuck you." The mechanic crawled from under the engine compartment and started wiping his hands, grumbling.

That was what Billy meant, but surely the man had to know that it would take a while to train the next mechanic. Billy watched the man storm out, neither saying anything else.

"You have to know that you're getting older? Don't you want to stand back and teach a younger generation?" Billy told the retreating figure, knowing that the mechanic couldn't hear him.

Billy didn't understand what happened, but it made him think. What if someone brought that up to him? What would have happened to New Boulder if Marcus had killed him?

Although Billy didn't intend to die anytime soon, it would take him a while to pass on what he learned in his life.

"I wonder how Felicity will be as a mother?" he asked himself out loud, thinking she may not go along with his newly discovered desire for an heir. That could be a rough conversation. He would have to make sure the windows were closed so they didn't entertain the guards out front while Billy was getting neutered. He cringed at the thought.

"Maybe she'll take it well," he said, trying to comfort himself.

CHAPTER FOURTEEN

James watched the colonel and the major as the group pushed on. Wherever they had gone on the break, something had changed between them. When they returned, the colonel was distant and short. The major was pleasant enough, but she couldn't seem to take her eyes from Terry Henry.

James figured they had a fight. He didn't know much about relationships. His parents were inseparable all the way to their deaths. Once he arrived in Brownsville, he didn't see anything that looked like a normal relationship. Some of the oldsters talked about being married and settling down. They talked as if it were heaven.

He'd been watching Terry and Char, the colonel and the major, and considered them to be as close as two human beings could be. He hoped they weren't fighting, that could make a long trip pretty miserable. He had so much to learn while on the road.

James sidled up next to the colonel during one of the walking phases of the travel. Thirty-thirty, he called it. Thirty minutes running and thirty minutes walking. James didn't know how he determined the time, but when he waved them to run, they kicked the horses into a trot that devoured distance without wearing the horses down, then they'd walk to rest, while continuing to cover ground.

They'd left the road and were traveling in the trickle of a river that was the South Platte. They watered the horses often, but didn't let them graze as much as Gerry wanted. He conceded for the moment, but insisted they find a good place when they settled in for the night and give the horses the opportunity to eat to their hearts' content.

"Thanks for bringing me along," James started. Terry nodded and looked at the young man. "I would like to know about training. We're going to do an awful lot of riding, and I get that, but I have a lot to learn. I don't want to waste any of the time I get to spend with you guys."

Terry looked across the road at Char. She was sniffing the air and squinting toward the horizon. He hoped she found the scent of something they could eat. He was getting hungry while trying to ration his remaining stash of goodies from Margie Rose. They'd been on the road nearly a full day, and he'd only eaten two pieces of venison jerky and a roll, besides the big breakfast the old woman had prepared.

They needed to hunt. The horses needed to graze. And it was time to come clean with his people.

"Halt!" Terry yelled as he held up his hand. Char looked at him sharply.

"Prey?" he asked closer to a whisper. She nodded as they sat atop their horses, waiting. She climbed down and shifted her pistols on her hips. Terry pointed ahead and she disappeared into a nearby ravine at a dead run.

He knew that she had to be hungry after the earlier workout. Terry hoped that she'd catch something big. He held his finger up to his lips. "Make camp. Quiet now, until we know if the hunt was successful. James, set up a defensive perimeter and watch schedule, include the major and me. We all stand watch."

James turned his horse and slowly walked back to the others, letting them know that they were to set up camp.

Terry pointed to a spot against a bank, sheltered on three sides. "Make a fire in there so it can't be seen. Wait until dark to light it, shouldn't be too long now." James issued a couple orders, then joined Lacy, and they headed down the mostly-dry riverbed to gather driftwood.

Terry removed his and Char's saddles then listened to see if he could hear where she'd gone. Geronimo was taking care of the other six horses, while the others prepared the camp. The ammunition almost made Gerry's knees buckle when he lifted it from the pack horses. Heavy packs all, but they had more firepower than Terry thought they'd use. He hoped they wouldn't get into a firefight like that, but better to have the ammunition and not need it.

The squeal of a javelina or other wild pig came clearly from the direction that Char had gone. Then a second. Terry's mouth started to water. Roast pig sounded good. It took another forty-five minutes before Char arrived with one pig, cleaned and ready to roast.

"Are you good?" Terry asked cryptically with James and Lacy nearby and Devlin and Gerry standing on the bank, one on each side of the river.

She hesitated before answering, looking at the others.

"I'm good," she finally said.

Terry butchered the small pig so it would cook more quickly, then handed everyone a couple pointed sticks to cook their pieces. He didn't have the time or inclination to build a spit. Clyde was exhausted, barely able to lift his head after nearly a full day of running after the horses. Terry fed the dog plenty of meat and gave him a leg bone to chew on while they cooked the rest of the pig. Clyde fell asleep with the bone in his mouth.

They cooked in silence and when their dinner was ready, Terry called the others down, while Char took the watch. Only he and Char knew that she'd already eaten, but to the others, it looked like she was taking one for the team.

Terry ate quickly, wolfing down his portion while the other one he'd cooked stayed warm for anyone who wanted more.

"Have you heard of Werewolves?" he asked. No one had. "Wolves?"

They nodded, curious where he was going.

"A Werewolf is a person who can turn into a wolf, but a powerful wolf, one that normal weapons don't affect. That's why I told the guard in New Boulder to send that man-mountain Marcus after us. They couldn't fight him and win. He would kill them all and there would be nothing they could do about it. We're out here because he's chasing after his mate," he said.

They looked confused. Geronimo's eyes shot wide. "Char!" he exclaimed.

"That's right, the major is a Werewolf. And she's going to have to fight him. We will be of little help. While out here, she's going to train to get faster, stronger, and ready to take him on. She'll need all of our help. For now, I need you all to unload your weapons, lock the bolts to the rear. We can't have any accidents." The four young members of the Force sat there and looked from Terry to their rifles.

"What are you waiting for?" he growled. "I gave you an order." They jumped into action. Lacy ejected her round directly into the fire and Terry dove in after it, pulling a scorched hand out with the round. He tossed it to back to the private.

"Please be more careful next time," he grunted, cradling his arm as the nanocytes rushed into action. Lacy was shocked as she looked at the skin starting to bubble on two of Terry's fingers.

"Char! If you would be so kind," Terry said into the darkness. With a small avalanche of dirt and rocks, a massive, brown she-wolf slid down the hillside. She crouched and growled when she hit the river bed. Devlin jumped backward, tripped over the log he'd been sitting on, and landed flat on his back. James jumped up.

"Sit down!" Terry ordered in his commander's voice. "This is our secret and you must keep it. You cannot tell anyone, ever, on pain of banishment and death. Do you understand me?" They nodded, but that wasn't good enough.

"I need each of you to look me in the face and tell me that you will take this secret to your graves. James?" One by one they swore to keep Char's secret. She strolled around the fire, walking close to each member of the Force, sniffing them and intimidating them. They recognized her purple eyes and felt more at ease, though fear still gripped them.

They'd never imagined that something like that existed. Their worlds had been simple ones, where finding food and water was the major effort of the day.

Devlin returned to his seat and ran a hand down the she-wolf's side. She snarled at him and he pulled back. "Keep your hands off the major, please," Terry said, trying not to laugh. She walked around the circle and sat down, very dog-like, next to Terry Henry Walton, where she leaned so heavily against him that she almost knocked him off his log. He wrapped his arm around her to keep from falling and stayed in that position.

Devlin pointed at him. "The major?" Terry shook his head.

"I will protect her with my life," Terry told them. She nuzzled his head in reply. He breathed deeply of the fur around her ears, smelling some of Char, a little of Clyde, and even some of himself. She stood and shook, smacking Terry with her ears and snickering, then slunk off into the darkness.

Shortly, the human Char joined them, bumping Terry over on his log to take her own seat. She took the last skewer and nibbled at the meat, but wrinkled her nose and handed it to James, who looked at it longingly. He broke it into four pieces and handed it to his squad.

Terry approved.

"Load up and go back on watch. You know what the major looks like in wolf form. The other one will be all black and big, much bigger. Watch for him. The only thing you can do is shoot him often until we can get there. We have a couple tricks up our sleeves that may give us an advantage."

"Like what?" James asked.

❖ ❖ ❖

Marcus woke and it was already dark. He felt refreshed enough to hunt, so he changed into the great black Werewolf. He headed out, circling to find a scent, then circled further. When he found nothing, he returned for his clothes and carrying them in his mouth, he followed the cold scent of the horses along the riverbed.

He ran up the bank at regular intervals to listen and sniff the air. When he smelled the buffalo, he had to go after it. It was a long ways off, but it would give him the strength he needed to catch his wayward mate and destroy those who traveled with her.

Across a great area of devastation he ran. No water and years of excessive heat had turned the land rough. It was nothing more than dried mud, which helped him as he ran, adjusting as the breeze carried the smell of a herd. He ran and ran, going north, further and further. Another river with more water was there, grass and trees growing along its bank.

A small herd of buffalo grazed peacefully, unaware of the violence headed their way.

Marcus adjusted to come in from downwind. The darkness concealed his black form. As he approached, he surprised a number of sleeping buffalo. Those he saw grazing were in the minority. The greatest number had been laying down. He looked for a calf, found one next to its mother, and he leapt onto its back.

The buffalo panicked, running every which way as the calf tried to dislodge the wolf perched on its back. The mother ran off with the others, leaving Marcus to finish his kill and begin the feast.

❖ ❖ ❖

James shook Terry Henry awake at what seemed like the middle of the night. "What happened?" he asked, brain fogged by the deep slumber from which he'd been roused.

"Nothing, sir. It's your watch, now till morning. You and

the major," he whispered. Terry blinked to clear his eyes, finding Char wrapped in his blanket with her head on his chest. His shirt and the cool of the night protected him from the Werewolf's heat. James dutifully avoided looking at how the two were intertwined.

Terry shook her, but she rolled over, pulling the covers tightly around her. "I'll stand watch alone," he told them, hating to change the plan because it seemed like he'd ordered them to do one thing while doing something else himself. "Belay that. Come on, Char, time to get up."

She didn't move, so he grabbed her shoulders and bodily picked her up, grunting with the effort. She was much denser than your average human. Terry ducked quickly, having seen her react before when getting wakened from a sound sleep.

Her elbow shot out with a hip twist to add power, just missing Terry's head. He caught it to keep her from rotating backward in a counter blow. She struggled awake, staggered two steps away, and puked.

"That's new," he said, looking at her.

"I feel awful," she said. "Oh no…"

Terry rushed forward and wrapped his arms around her, stroking her hair, concern contorting his face.

She leaned close. "Going into heat," she whispered. Terry stepped back, trying not to smile or panic.

"Umm," was all he managed to say while looking everywhere but at her.

"Uh-huh," she replied, glaring at him. "Just go away. I'll deal with you later."

Terry had no idea what that meant, but he had no intention of staying around to find out. He did the appropriately manly thing and ran for his life.

❖ ❖ ❖

"My dearest Felicity, I've been thinking," Billy started in a soft voice, smiling. Felicity was instantly skeptical.

"Now that sounds dangerous, Billy dear," Felicity drawled, pulling the covers closer around her. "So what have you been thinking about?"

"The person who will take my place after I get old and pack it in," he replied. He got ready to continue, but Felicity cut him off.

"Oh, Billy! I never thought you'd think of me as the next mayor! I am flattered and simply overwhelmed. I don't know what to say, but I know how I can show my appreciation." Her voice dropped to a whisper as she crawled under the covers. The touch of her warm fingers convinced Billy that he shouldn't continue with his previous train of thought.

That's not what I meant, he thought, shaking his head and shelving the idea for the present. Maybe after he had her in his car…

CHAPTER FIFTEEN

The false dawn was a welcome sight. Terry woke Geronimo to help him saddle the horses after Terry brought them together from grazing the riverbank. He hoped they had enough to eat and looked to Gerry for confirmation. The young man stroked their sides and then nodded.

"My pretty girls have had plenty," he said happily, throwing a saddle onto one's back and cinching it tightly. Then moving to the next. Terry lifted the ammunition-heavy saddle bags and put them on the two horses who wouldn't carry riders that day. He and Char rode the same horses day after day because they were used to the Werewolf, while the others were still skittish around her.

The others roused, packed up, and prepared to leave.

"Char," Terry called quietly. She materialized from the shadows and approached.

"Wow, you look normal!" he blurted out.

"Why wouldn't I?" she asked. He realized his mistake too late, but he was a warrior, honed to a fine edge in battles past. He redirected.

"Is that Marcus?" he whispered. Char knew the alpha Werewolf wasn't anywhere near, so she shook her head.

"We better go, keep on keeping on, and maybe we'll find a settlement of some sort today. It'd be nice to accomplish the secondary mission of recruiting more bodies for New Boulder." He raised his eyebrows and nodded. He walked away with a sense of urgency, hurriedly mounting his horse and waving the others to follow.

A Marine Corps lesson was to always look like you know what you're doing and to do it like there is nothing more important at the moment. A busy Marine was a happy Marine, or so the leadership believed. If one didn't look busy enough…

Clyde ran around looking for a place to go, so they all waited while the dog took care of business. As soon as he was done, Clyde did like all dogs and took off running.

Too bad it was in the wrong direction. Terry yelled at him until he turned and followed as they spurred their horses east toward the rising sun.

"When will you know if Marcus is following us?" Terry asked in a whisper.

"When he's a few miles away. We won't get much in the way of a heads up," she replied. "I don't sense anything, and riding into the wind doesn't help. If he's back there, he'll find us before we find him."

"That's not quite the tactical position I was looking for." Terry stroked his chin with one hand, feeling the stubble as he thought. He hadn't shaved, opting to wear enough stubble to keep his face warm. It would only get colder, although the cold of the Wasteland already felt far warmer than the cold of New Boulder. He wondered what the climate was like, how it had changed in the past twenty years. He knew the baseline because he'd read the reports before the World's Worst Day Ever, the WWDE.

He had no way to measure current temperatures to tell what the difference might be, but that wasn't the same. He couldn't get the average over a large area. He expected that his body had adapted and the climate was warmer overall. Did it snow out here? It probably didn't anymore.

His curiosity piqued, he thought he'd look for a thermometer. If he could find one, he'd start taking the temperature as they passed through areas. He missed his studies. The world had been without academic research for too long.

"What was your major, Ivy League?" Terry asked.

"Ivy League? Leave it to a Marine to call it that. I majored in history," she answered.

He grunted.

"What? Were you hoping for something else?" she retorted.

"No, not at all. I studied history as well. Love that stuff! Do you know anything about hard science, say, climatology?" he clarified.

"Yes. I had a boyfriend who was a weatherman on TV. He tried to convince me that he wasn't just guessing. The jury is still out on that, although I recognized that with good data, the quality of the predictions improves. The challenge now is we have no data and no way to get it."

"I think we can find a thermometer," Terry offered.

"A thermometer? That's your idea of data?" She paused a moment, taking it in. "I guess it's better than nothing, but if we can find an all-in-one weather station, then maybe, just maybe, we can start to figure things out. Wait!" Char sat up straight and sniffed the air. The wind had changed and was blowing from the northwest.

"Marcus is coming," Char whispered. Terry turned and looked, but the sun had not yet tipped from night. "He's a long ways away and I smell something else, cows maybe? I think he just hunted. We need to hurry."

The sun peeked over the horizon, starting its climb skyward. The barren land before them was disheartening. It appeared from the shadows, looking worse as it became better lit. When the sun stepped away from the land, the way ahead looked as bad as it could be. From the ditch of the South Platte River, sparse greenery fought against the blood red of the waste.

Terry stopped, picked Clyde up, and carried the poor dog, who was already struggling to keep up.

"We need to move!" Terry called to the others, not worried that he'd be heard because of the wind's new direction. Terry kicked his horse into a trot, then a run as they sought the best footing through the Wastelands. Keeping the South Platte close on their left side, they raced ahead, covering as much distance as possible in the cool of the morning.

When the wind changed direction again, Char lost all traces of the other Werewolf, but Terry was pleased regardless.

"He could not have spent any time in town if he's close enough for you to smell him. That's exactly what we wanted, but now that we know he's coming, I feel good, excited even," Terry confided. Char looked at him in surprise.

"You should be afraid," she replied, face twisted, but her purple eyes almost glowed as energy surged within her.

"Save that!" Terry cautioned. "Funnel your emotions at the proper time. Focus the rage and use it to your advantage. He will be angry and out of control. We'll use that against him as long as we get to pick the terrain of the battle. That's my job. Yours is to practice and run and get faster and faster."

Char looked at the wasted land ahead, wondering how in the hell Terry Henry Walton was going to find terrain to their advantage.

Terry figured the right battleground was on the other side of the great waste before them, hoping for more fertile land in what used to be Nebraska. He wanted to be there before nightfall, a good seventy-five miles from where they'd camped. If Marcus had run the whole way, he'd have to be tired. And that would be an advantage, too.

Char looked back as the sun painted the world behind them a deep red. She couldn't see anything and couldn't sense that he was close, but ahead, she felt the life essence of humans and livestock.

❖ ❖ ❖

"Billy, I think we need to do a recon, go north and check things out, make sure that man has moved on," Mark suggested.

"Did Terry Henry give you that much freedom? Does that make sense in any way?" Billy shot back. He'd been happy that Marcus left town without wreaking havoc, but he still didn't want to see any more members of the security team disappear. Billy had already lost his security chief, Char, four others, and eight horses.

At least he had faith that they would return if they were able to. He hoped they would bring more people. Billy laughed to himself, still greedy after all these years, but for different things. He wanted a thriving city with a restaurant and music, drinks besides Terry's god-awful beer.

And a car, but he was doing a lot of the work himself…if

only he could get the mechanic back on board. The older man was still angry. In the old days, a gentle beating would have done the trick, but Billy was out of people who would deliver those. He couldn't send Felicity to apologize since she didn't know about the car.

A quandary, but if that was the worst problem Billy Spires, Mayor of New Boulder had, then life was pretty good.

"Day trip only, I think you'll learn enough from that. And just two people and two horses. We have limited logistics and can risk no more than that. What would your people do if they came across that man, or others, for that matter?"

"Our rules of engagement? Run. Return to town with the information. It's a recon, not a search and destroy or move-ment to contact," Mark said, proud that he'd remembered the terms Terry had used when they traveled south to Browns-ville.

"When do you want to do this?"

"Tomorrow, and the two-man guard remains in place at all times. That won't stop. Thanks, Billy. We won't let you down," Mark declared.

Mark stood, lacking anything else to say, while Billy had always been a man of few words. Felicity was sitting on her couch, reading a book, a rare pleasure that few people had the time or energy for.

When Mark walked out into the morning sun and a cool breeze, he shivered and pulled his rough coat more tightly around himself.

I won't let you down, either, Colonel Walton, Mark vowed.

Mark had been ten on the WWDE. His family was from right there in Boulder. They hunkered down in a hunting cab-in in the hills, occasionally returning to town to watch how fast civilization deteriorated. That was how he lost his mom, to a gang when she simply hoped to find some cold medicine for her son.

The gang spotted her and ran her over with their motorcycles. Mark's dad found her the next day. She hadn't returned, so he went looking for her. The old man was never the same after that. He taught Mark to read, to hunt using snares and deadfalls and at rare times, to shoot the family hunting rifle. They didn't have very much ammunition, so Mark's dad allocated five rounds a year to kill an elk or a large deer in order to have enough meat to last until the next hunt.

When is one hundred rounds of ammunition for your high-powered rifle not enough? When you're ten years old and it has to last a lifetime.

Mark watched his dad die when he fell from a rocky hillside. Mark had been a teenager. He took the rifle and the remaining ammunition and walked into New Boulder. Billy Spires had taken the rifle away from the boy, but gave him something to eat and a place to stay. He'd been put in John's charge.

At first, Mark had enjoyed the power that John wielded over others, but it never made him comfortable. When Terry Henry Walton showed up, Mark saw a different way, a better way. John had never been a leader. Billy, on the other hand, despite his self-serving nature, was a leader who people followed. And now, Mark actually enjoyed talking with the man. Which reminded Mark of something, taking a lesson from Terry.

He returned to Billy's house, knocked, listened carefully for the yell to enter, then walked a few steps inside.

"I forgot something I've been meaning to tell you, Billy. Thank you for taking me in all those years ago. You helped me become the man I am today. I don't want you to think I'm ungrateful." Mark nodded as he finished and quickly excused himself.

Billy turned to Felicity, who had looked up from her book. "What do you think that was all about?"

"Well, Billy dear, the people are thankful for what you've done to build a stable community. I'm proud of you, Billy," Felicity said, her southern accent lighter than usual, her voice low.

Billy lost himself. "Let's have kids!" The words came out in a rush and he froze as Felicity slowly lowered her book and peered at him over the top. Her eyes gave nothing away.

"Billy dear, there are a lot of steps between this and that," she replied.

"I like those steps." Billy smiled and nodded.

"Mmmhmmm," Felicity mumbled as her eyes disappeared behind her book, and she returned to reading.

The cat was out of the bag, and Billy wasn't sure if he was in the doghouse or not.

❖ ❖ ❖

The day was a blur. The dust that Terry and Char kicked up had been burning the eyes of those behind. They decided to ride six abreast, which slowed them a little but not enough to keep them from tearing across the Wastelands. They'd whip in to the river every hour, but wouldn't dismount as the horses drank their fill. At midday, they stopped at a place where they could shelter the horses in a ravine. Terry set up an obstacle course for Char and included the other four. Their job was to throw blocks of wood at her head and her job was to catch them.

Lacy held up a blanket as Char disrobed and changed into a Werewolf. Then she was off, running up and down the cut through which the trickle of a river traveled.

As she flew past the members of the force, they tried throwing things at her, but she was too fast. Their efforts resulted in wood flying far behind her. Then Char took to running straight at them, where their aim vastly improved, although the humans skinned knees and hands from diving out of the way of a rampaging Werewolf. Terry yelled encouragement the whole time, snapping his whip for effect.

Clyde howled and decided to run back and forth instead of trying to futilely chase the much faster Were.

After thirty minutes, Terry called a halt. Lacy and Char reversed the process, and the major emerged from behind the blanket, dressed and breathing heavily. They hadn't eaten, but Terry told them to mount their horses and get ready to go.

"We have a lot more work to do," he told Char. She nodded. She could feel it, too. "Which means we need to buy ourselves more time."

They headed back into the Wastelands, urging their mounts to greater and greater speed, staying as close to the river as possible as it was cooler closer to the water. They weren't that far from Boulder, as the crow flew, but they felt like they were in the middle of a desert's summer. It was late fall.

"There are people up ahead," Char said matter-of-factly.

The Wastelands will be impassable for most of the year. How in the hell did you people survive out here? Terry wondered as they approached a group of buildings in the middle of nowhere.

❖ ❖ ❖

Marcus awoke in the late morning, feeling much like his old self. Strong with a great deal of energy. He ate more of the calf and with his clothes bundle in his great jaws, he headed southeast in search of the river.

He ran through the scrub and parched, dry land, wondering how long he was going to pursue Charumati. The cool of the mountains called to him.

But to give up the chase would be to admit defeat. He couldn't do that, and the strange human, Terry Henry Walton, needed to die. Marcus plowed ahead, with less than complete conviction. The hard and hot ground was hurting his paws.

That made him angry.

"Char!" he bellowed as a Werewolf growl. He stopped and howled at the cloudless sky, before digging in and running again.

The heat pounded down on him, but he kept going. When he spotted the green of trees and bushes, he angled directly toward them. He didn't hesitate when he cleared the bank and dove into the cut, finding the deepest hole of water and submerging himself.

He crawled out of the river's pool and headed upstream to get a drink, then he sniffed the ground, looking for her scent. He left the river and headed into the waste. The trail the horses left was clearly visible. They paralleled the river and he could see their track leading far into the distance. He put his nose to the ground and breathed deeply.

At least a day old, maybe more. He studied the hoof prints. The horses were running.

Marcus growled his pleasure. They were running for their lives.

He couldn't wait to catch them. *By running, you will only die tired*, he thought.

Marcus flowed across the ground like windblown dust. He barely touched the dirt as he stretched to his full length, lunging ahead and using his body efficiently as he ran–push, pull, glide.

He would catch them. If not today, then tomorrow, but no later than the next day. Even an infant could follow the trail they were leaving.

Marcus was no infant. He could feel the smoke pouring from his ears like from the funnel of an old steam engine. The Werewolf alpha let the rage smolder, stoking it just enough to keep his speed up.

Soon, bitch, soon.

CHAPTER SIXTEEN

Terry ordered the Force to spread out, to be harder targets if the Wasteland settlers happened to be armed. He let Clyde slide to the ground to run alongside the horses. As they closed in on the buildings, Terry took one last look behind to make sure they wouldn't get surprised by Marcus in the middle of a first contact.

He couldn't see anything. Char shook her head, confirming that the alpha wasn't close.

Terry raised a fist, calling a halt when they were fifty feet from what looked like a main building. It was one of seven, all perched on the bank of the South Platte. Cattle grazed on the other side of the river in a fenced enclosure that opened to a long stretch along the river with trees and grass. It looked like an oasis.

The building's door was thrown open and a man stepped out, brandishing a shotgun. "We have nothing for you here.

Go away!" he bellowed as he tried to look menacing. He was older, walking with a heavy limp. His gnarled hands held the rusty weapon that probably hadn't been fired in years.

"We are no threat to you, good sir," Terry called out, holding his hands up. "I think we may have something to offer you, though." Clyde barked and ran toward the man, tail wagging.

The old man watched the dog approach, then took a knee as Clyde made a new friend. "Been a while since I seen a dog. I'm Antioch Weathers. Who might you be?"

Terry nodded to Char and they both dismounted while the others stayed back. "I'm Terry Henry Walton and this is Charumati," Terry said, smiling as he approached, careful to not hold his rifle as he normally would. When Terry held out his hand, the old man took it, his dark skin contrasting with Terry's well-tanned hands.

Antioch looked at Char, surprised showing on his face. "My. Had I known there were people like you out there, I would have searched the Wastelands to my dying breath."

"I thank you, but we live in the foothills, outside of what used to be Boulder, and that's what we're here to offer you," Char said smoothly. Antioch turned his head, ears perked up. He leaned into the doorway and yelled for everyone to come out.

Young people of all ages, from small children to those in their early twenties, appeared one by one, coming out to stare at the newcomers. The last one out, wearing an apron and carrying a wooden spoon, looked to be Antioch's wife as she took a position at his side, holding tightly to his arm.

Terry started to laugh. Antioch's eyes narrowed. Char turned to him as if he'd gone mad. The horses shifted while Clyde bounced from one person to the next, knocking over the smallest where the two began to wrestle.

"I'm sorry. I saw that wooden spoon and thought of old Margie Rose, the kindest woman I've ever met. She lets Char and I stay with her in New Boulder. She carries a wooden spoon, too, and I've been on the wrong end of it, more than once." Terry smiled broadly, disarmingly.

"Me, too," Char admitted.

The old woman slapped Antioch. "Oh! My wife, Claire, and these are our children. Yes, you see it right. Twelve boys. Not a single young lady anywhere and here you are with two!" Claire reached up and smacked her husband on the head with her spoon. He winced and tried to get away, but she hung onto him.

"What my husband meant to say is, welcome to our home. You said you could do something for us?" Claire asked.

"We need people in New Boulder. We have greenhouses and fertile fields. We have a power plant that generates electricity using natural gas from a local well. We have one hundred thirty, one hundred forty people? But we are expanding and need more," Terry claimed, talking animatedly with his hands as he delivered his best sales pitch.

"Your cattle could form a new and incredible herd. Your experience with them and your willingness to work, judging by your calloused hands, will make you welcome additions. Our goal in coming into the Wastelands was to find other survivors and offer them the opportunity to move to New Boulder, help us rebuild civilization. We'll show you the way there, if you're interested."

Antioch turned to Claire, then back to Terry. "It's been a hard year and they seem to keep getting harder. We used to have so many more cattle. This is all that's left. Summers are hard here." The old man hesitated and looked into the distance. "We'll need to talk amongst ourselves, but it would be nice to sleep without sweating, eat something that I didn't have to kill or grow myself, but we built all this, kept it going for the past twenty years. I'd hate to give it up on a fool's quest."

Antioch stood proudly, his family at his side.

Terry's plan was to funnel people back toward New Boulder, staying along the river and following the tracks and trail that the FDG had made on their way out. With Marcus following, did he want to send people right into him? Terry found himself wondering what the right answer was.

"We'll wait out here. Is there a place where we can water the horses?" A young man waved Terry around the western side of the house and pointed to a cut, where there was a gentle decline to the river. It was above where any of the cattle's waste made its way into the South Platte River.

Gerry led the way with the horses as James tapped his rifle while looking at Terry. The colonel shook his head and waved them away. There was no threat here. Lacy took the reins of Char's horse and James took Terry's.

"What will Marcus do if he comes across this bunch as they're making their way west?" Terry asked Char when they were alone.

"I'd like to think that he'll continue after us. We just need them to deliver the message to him, just like our people must have done in New Boulder. If he comes this far, he won't be distracted by this family. They are no threat to him, but if he's hungry, then they may lose a cow. Let's say I hope he would go after a cow and not one of the children," she whispered and made sure she wasn't overheard.

"We water and feed the horses, give Antioch and Claire directions, then we move on. No matter what we do after this, that family will get to meet Marcus. By being just ahead of him, he'll have to keep coming. It doesn't seem in his nature to give up, not now, not after coming all this way. We need to be close enough where he can't delay, but far enough where he still has to work to get to us. I'm sorry, Char, but we're going to have to fight him before we're ready," Terry said, looking at the ground.

Char pulled Terry close and hugged him, resting her head on his shoulder. He breathed deeply of her hair, wondering how it always smelled like it did, even when traveling in the dust and dirt of the Wastelands.

Someone cleared their throat. Terry and Char hurriedly stepped apart.

"I wouldn't let go of that one, either, if I was you, young man. I don't blame you in the least. We'll go, but we'd like you to come with us, show us the way," Antioch offered, hope in his eyes.

"I'm sorry, but we simply cannot. We have a ways to go and there's one other thing. There's a man chasing us and we can't let him catch us out here. When you see him, whether it is here or as you're following the river west, tell him where we've gone, even if he doesn't ask. Point him in our direction," Terry replied.

"I can't say I'm too pleased with all that, not sure why you'd lead someone who's chasing you straight to us. Maybe you can hook me up with one of those pop guns of yours," Antioch said coldly.

"These won't matter with him. Don't be a threat to him and he should leave you alone. He's after her." Terry pointed as he appealed to Antioch's sense of male honor.

"You look like a fighter, but you're running from this guy. Why?"

"We need to finish him where none of his followers can find his body," Terry replied, curling his lip into a snarl.

"Ha!" Antioch exclaimed and slapped the larger Terry Henry on the back as he returned to the house. Terry and Char followed as they wanted everyone in that family to understand clearly that they needed to send Marcus after Char.

❖ ❖ ❖

Timmons stood on the terrazzo of what used to be the Air Force Academy. He was surprised that most of the spires of the iconic chapel had survived the blasts and the years since. The rough marble of the areas around the chapel and the parade deck of the main courtyard between the dormitories was almost completely overgrown and now teemed with wildlife.

Deer had always been prevalent on the old Academy grounds, but now, they seemed to have taken over. Timmons wondered where the predators had gone.

The other predators, he thought, then nodded to the pack. They shed their clothes and changed into Werewolf form. They ran low, below the cover of the wall along the upper grounds. There were wide steps at either end that led to the former parade ground.

Timmons watched, as if he were in a zoo.

The pack slinked down the steps and disappeared into the overgrowth on both sides of the massive park-like area. The Werewolves converged and charged. Deer bolted in all directions, some into the attacking predators, some away. Each of his people found a mark, some running for longer than others after their prey, but none of them were denied.

Timmons became a Werewolf and with his paws on the top of the wall, he looked down at the pack, now scattered around the area and feasting on their kills.

Every single day, he regretted leaving Marcus alive. He'd told them that when Marcus found them, he'd kill one or two as an example to the others, but they couldn't do it, even though Marcus had gone off the rails a long time before.

Timmons was living on borrowed time. He would be the first to die if Marcus found them.

"I can't live my life in fear!" he howled at the old parade deck. Then began talking to himself as he strolled to find some venison to dine on. "We eat and then let's find us a place to stay. It looks like it could take a while to explore here. I wonder if the old labs have anything worthwhile left. It's been a while since I brewed anything fun."

Timmons had been an engineer in the before time, but he liked playing with the chemicals, especially when they could make explosives. Merrit had been a chemist. Between the two of them, Timmons had high hopes they could make something that would be entertaining. Maybe it was time for the chapel's spires to come down.

Or time to build something that could kill a Werewolf, because Timmons couldn't beat Marcus all by himself. A little help in the form of the terrorist-favorite, homemade explosive TATP?

Well, shit. That could make all the difference.

❖ ❖ ❖

After having a good dinner of beef and green beans, Terry gave Antioch and Claire the directions to New Boulder. Along with the others, Terry thanked the couple for the meal, gave his regards, and ordered the members of the FDG to mount up.

They waved goodbye in appreciation of a good, home-cooked meal, then headed east, following the river's course.

Terry spurred his horse to a gallop and off they went.

"We need to make up some ground," he said into the wind. Clyde lay across his lap, whining in discomfort.

"I know," Char answered, leaning into the horse's neck as it ran. For thirty minutes he let the horses run, then he slowed them to a walk, then another thirty minutes of running.

Geronimo puked during the second run, but he didn't complain.

James wondered about the hurry. They had yet to do any training, and he wondered if they'd ever get to it.

Lacy kept her eye on James while Devlin just tried to stay upright in the saddle. It was a motley group, but the best one that Terry could cobble together. Each had their own skill, but he wondered if they'd get a chance to demonstrate what they were good at. Two mechanically-inclined, but there were no towns out here, no place to set a mechanical trap.

Terry had hoped they'd corner the great Werewolf and with a trap or two, hurt him badly enough that Char could finish him.

"We're going to have to do it the hard way," Terry said out loud during the short interval the horses were walking.

"I'm sorry, I must have missed the plan that wasn't the hard way," Char said humorlessly.

"It was a long shot, but I was hoping to sucker Marcus into a small town where we'd be able to trap him, injure him as much as possible. I have a couple bullets which have silver rubbed on them, my silvered knife, and now my bullwhip, but I don't expect him to stand still while I take aim or run through my weapons. So I'm going to have to get real close and unload on him. I know that hope is a lousy plan, but I hope that distracts him enough for you to take him out," Terry stated.

"TH, always so chivalrous. What if I don't want your protection, my big, tough human?"

Terry looked at her sideways. "You have to be kidding! My goal is to survive, all of us live to see tomorrow. We fight him however we can. I just wanted to put our options on the table, that's all. And I can't think of anything else. No matter what, my mind keeps coming back to Marcus."

"It's supposed to. He's the alpha, and that's how alphas like it. He has you right where he wants you, afraid and running for your life," Char told him.

"Maybe that's what we've been doing wrong," Terry started, his mind racing anew. "We could have trapped him in that first place we stopped outside of New Boulder. Why wouldn't that have worked? Because I fixed in my mind that we needed to drag him way the hell out into this god-forsaken fucking waste of a land."

"You told Billy Spires that you were going to look for people. You told Margie Rose that you wanted her to live in peace. Maybe you're trying to do too much, keep your word to too many different people," she offered.

What Char told him rang true. When he returned to humanity, he committed his entire being to saving them. Every minute of his day was spent in that pursuit. Sawyer Brown was an inconvenience that Terry was well-equipped to deal with. Marcus, on the other hand, represented the horrors of the WWDE, the helplessness of a world spinning out of control.

His inability to save his family.

So he took Char and ran, justifying it in his own mind as

the right thing to do to save the people of New Boulder.

He stopped his horse, signaling to the others to halt. He nudged his horse next to Char's so he could face her. "When did you know?" he asked.

"When did I know what?" she whispered.

"All of it," he added cryptically.

"When you kicked Clyde off the bed to be closer to me." She smiled at him, her purple eyes sparkling.

"What? Clyde? You based your perception of our relationship entirely on Clyde?" Terry turned his head sideways, not unlike the dog that pranced around the horses, happy for the respite.

"You love that dog." She smiled.

Terry leaned close. "I do," he answered softly, before leaning back and shouting. "Now, what do you say we go kill us a fucking alpha? Come on, Clyde!"

Terry spurred his horse forward, turned in a tight circle to face east, then waved his arm over his head. With her ears flattened against her head, Terry's mare bolted forward, sending dust clouds into her wake as the others raced to catch up.

CHAPTER SEVENTEEN

Mark and Boris rode north, past the power plant and into the ruins of suburb after suburb. They saw the charcoal mark on the ground where Terry and his people had turned toward Longmont. The two continued along the remains of that highway until it crossed the South Platte River.

Another mark on the ground pointed in a new direction.

Mark and Boris dismounted, tying their horses to an old light pole. They saw the hoof prints as the eight horses entered the dirt of the mostly dry river bed. That was only partly what Mark was looking for.

He didn't find any human footprints, only those of massive paws which seemed bigger than the hoof prints.

"What do you make of these?" Mark asked. Boris looked closely, moving from one to the next. He jumped between them, trying to get an idea how big the animal was.

"This can't be a dog. A bear, maybe?" Boris suggested

Mark shook his head. Bears had five toes and a pronounced claw at the tip of each. This was the paw of a canine. "I think it's a wolf, but I've never seen anything this size before." Mark stomped around, torn over what to do as indecision gripped him.

"Fucking whore!" Mark yelled.

Boris jumped, looking around as if they were getting ambushed. He looked down the sights of his rifle as he scanned the nearby buildings.

"Hey! What if that thing is nearby? Fuck, man! Don't call down the thunder just 'cause you're pissed," Boris said, one hand out trying to calm the corporal.

"We have to follow them, but we can't. We have to go back, but we shouldn't," Mark argued with himself.

"If it helps, I don't see any human footprints. We need to take that information back. That man is running around somewhere out here, but I don't see where he's following them," Boris said, shining the light on what Mark was missing.

"Holy shit! We have to go back, but let's run up the river for a while, see if he jumped in at a different spot, but then we have to tell Billy." Mark ran up the riverbank, untied his horse, and jumped into the saddle. He navigated the riverbank while Boris was still trying to mount his ride.

He hurried after Mark, trying to look at every building window, behind every mound of dirt for the boogeyman who was out there somewhere. And then there was a massive beast, large as a horse and running after their people. But, it was Terry Henry Walton on the other end of that chase.

Maybe you don't want to catch up to them, Boris thought. He suddenly heard a noise and studied the landscape to try and figure out what the sound was and where it came from. Mark pushed forward, oblivious to everything else except the tracks.

Who's hunting whom? Boris asked himself.

❖ ❖ ❖

Marcus continued to run, feeling strong after eating the buffalo calf. His rage consumed him, and he ran, hard, taking few breaks to drink and cool down.

He sensed something far ahead. People and cattle, walking toward him. He'd prefer to just run past, but being seen as a Werewolf wasn't something he wanted to do. There was only one thing he was afraid of–the Forsaken. They didn't care about much of what he did, but revealing the existence of the Were world was taboo.

It would get the skin flayed off him. His pain and ultimate death would give the Forsaken much pleasure, but having to go after the tainted humans and kill them all? The Forsaken would find that a huge pain in the ass, so they'd make Marcus suffer all the more.

No. He wanted to, because he knew he was catching up to them. No horse could outrun him. They were too weak. After killing the humans and conquering his mate, he'd dine on one of their mounts, maybe kill them all out of spite. He relished the thought.

He changed into human form, put on his clothes, and jogged up the riverbed where the approaching group couldn't see how fast he was running.

As he closed on them, he slowed, then jumped into the stream. Dripping wet, he staggered up the bank and threw himself onto the ground.

The group of people stopped and looked at him in shock.

"Where did you come from?" an old man asked, his wife at his side along with an array of children from five to twenty. A small herd of cows followed obediently.

"I've been following my wife, she has purple eyes, and an interloper, a family wrecker!" Marcus howled, pleading with the patriarch and matriarch of the family before him. The old lady hurried to him to help him up.

He stood, towering over the little old lady. She gasped and backed away. The old man fingered his rusty shotgun as he looked at the massive human being who stood before them. The younger children hid behind their parents. The only ones unimpressed were the cows, who continued ambling west.

Antioch remembered himself and did as Terry Henry Walton had asked.

"They are going east, following the river. You'll see our place a ways back. Keeping going past that. You can't miss their tracks. She's with them, as you already know," Antioch intoned, sounding as if he'd memorized the script.

Marcus reached out with his senses. Maybe, kind of, almost at the edge of what he could feel. Char and something else. He needed to get closer.

"Thank you, kind people. I'll be on my way, if you don't mind." Marcus dismissed the group, assuming they'd die in the Wastelands before they could get wherever they were going. He looked longingly at the cows as he ran past, but he'd be dining on fresh horse meat before too long. Marcus ran ahead, checking back every now and then to see the group fade into the distance. When they could no longer see, he removed his clothes and changed into a Werewolf. He ran to the river, dunked his head, drank deeply, and raced back up the bank. The cows had obliterated the hoof prints he'd been following, but that didn't matter. He could see where they'd gone and soon, he'd catch them.

There was *nowhere* to hide in the Wastelands.

Terry Henry Walton's heart ripped from his chest, Marcus chewing it casually as the flies gathered around the dead man. Horseflesh, raw, blood still pumping, and his mate, cowering at his feet and licking the blood from his fur if that's what he commanded her to do.

Soon, all would be right with his world.

Then he'd find those other traitorous fucks of his pack and make them lick their own blood from his paws.

❖ ❖ ❖

Terry pushed the group hard as he searched for the right place. As nightfall approached on the day after leaving Antioch and Claire's homestead, he wondered if they'd misjudged Marcus. He instantly learned that he hadn't.

"He is coming," Char told the group as they attempted to make a fire in a ravine leading from the river.

"How long do we have?" Terry asked.

"A half-hour, maybe less. He is moving with a great deal of determination, it seems," Char said calmly.

"Gerry, hide the horses up the river. James and Devlin, set up on the opposite riverbank. Lacy, down here with us. You'll have the best angle to shoot, if we can get him to come down the river. Stoke that fire! We need something to draw him here and you need to be able to see your target," Terry ordered, running downriver to find more driftwood to use as kindling. He returned with an armload as did the others. They lit it and stoked it to make one grand bonfire.

The light blazed into the dark of the early night. The heat was too much to stand close.

"Get in position now, hurry up," Terry told them. He heard one of the horses whinny. "Farther away, Geronimo!" he called, cupping his hands around his mouth to yell downriver.

"That's it? Your plan is we draw him in here and then stand side by side as he kills us both?" Char said with a half-smile.

Clyde laid down by the fire, anxious at the activity and the emotions surging through the alpha and the others.

"No. I was going to stand over there, so I don't get any of your blood on me. It would be so hard to get out of my uniform," he quipped. She only shook her head as he moved away and double-checked the two silvered bullets in his rifle. He removed the sling and held the rifle free. He loosened his knife and wrapped his bullwhip around his forearm.

Then they waited.

Char moved aside, undressed, and changed into her Werewolf form. She stretched and snarled. Then she reared back and howled her challenge to the night sky.

A howl responded from the distance.

❖ ❖ ❖

"We lost that man Marcus, Billy, and to add insult to injury, some beast is following the colonel. An hour's ride down the river and its tracks were right there on top of the hoof prints.. We had to come back, let you know that the man didn't follow them. We don't know where he went," Mark stated, trying not to look like he'd failed, although that was exactly what he felt.

"Isn't that what you went out there for, to find out?" Billy asked as he leaned back in his chair. "So if that man comes back, we finish him, without talking. We'll call Terry's plan to lead him away a nice try, but we'll take care of it ourselves, don't you think, Mark?"

"That works for me. I'd like to go back out there, keep looking, if I may," Mark asked.

"No." Billy leaned forward, putting his forearms on the table. "You found out what you could, and now you need to set up the welcoming committee for when Marcus returns. No hesitation next time. We shoot to kill. Is that clear?" Mark nodded, pursing his lips. He looked to Billy for more, but there wasn't anything else.

Boris had been silent the entire time. He didn't have anything to add, and he definitely didn't want to skyline himself with the mayor. Sometimes, anonymity was a good thing.

Mark stood up, waved Boris to follow, and walked out to inform the men. He needed to make a plan that was counter to the colonel's last orders. He didn't like it, but that was the position he filled.

"Boris, go get everyone and then we'll build our trap. I wonder if Billy will let us put someone in his attic," he said, thinking out loud as Boris ran off to find the rest of the guard.

❖ ❖ ❖

"We stay here," Timmons told them, trying to exert his authority as the new alpha, a position that he thought of for himself. The others had followed, only thinking Timmons the senior beta, not an all-powerful alpha.

"We stay because we like it here, not because of your order," Sue countered, standing up straight, looking small compared to the males. The others nodded.

"Maybe it's time we decide?" Timmons pressed. Xandrie and Shonna leaned back as if they'd been punched. Sue sat down. She wasn't the one to challenge for the leadership of the pack.

Ted and Adams avoided looking at Timmons. Merrit stood up, put his hand on his chin, raised one eyebrow, and looked very much like the thinking man.

"Why?" Merrit asked simply.

"Because, the pack needs a leader!" Timmons retorted, working his anger, feeding it as he readied himself for the physical fight for dominance. Merrit held up his hands and shook his head.

"No one is going to fight you today, Timmons. We're staying. Is that not good enough? If you want to play alpha, more power to you, but what happens when Marcus returns? We will point to you and he will kill you, then we'll assume our roles as good betas. If he's convinced we don't have a new alpha, then maybe we all survive." Merrit talked while walking back and forth, reasoning out his argument.

"By leaving Marcus alive, we agreed that he was the alpha. A pack can't have two, Timmons, no matter how much we'd like to see you in that role." Merrit smiled as a way to solidify his point.

The others nodded.

"We should have killed him," Timmons snarled.

"There is no value in such recriminations, my friend," Merrit answered. "We have to live with our decisions. So, let's make the best of it. We stay. There's plenty of game. It's comfortable here. For now, let's call it home."

The others nodded again in agreement. Timmons was angry that Merrit was right. He took a deep breath and calmed himself. "Maybe we can dig something useful out of those labs. It'd be nice to blow shit up again. I miss that…"

CHAPTER EIGHTEEN

Terry moved to the other side of the small stream that trickled down the center of the riverbed. The South Platte had carried a great deal more water in the before time, but it had also run dry back then, too. At least there was some water and it wasn't tainted.

And none of that mattered in their current situation. The alpha bore down on them from the bank to their left, the south side of the river. Char stood closest to that point. Terry aimed his rifle at the bank, waiting for the moment the great black Werewolf appeared.

The rest of the Force were arrayed to bring maximum firepower to bear on the alpha and catch him in a crossfire, assuming he entered the riverbed where Char and Terry waited.

Char dropped to all fours and snarled. Her hackles rose and spittle flew from her mouth. Those on the banks were unnerved by the sight and the sound. The bonfire reflected off her shiny pelt. Lacy was on the south riverbank, and she was the first one to see him approach, only glimpses as he glided over the Wastelands in the weak moonlight.

Terry put Lacy there because he assumed the alpha wouldn't attack a woman.

Marcus unerringly bore down on Lacy. She fired, then panicked and flipped the lever to automatic. She yanked back on the trigger, spraying her rounds skyward as the barrel jumped. She emptied an entire magazine and didn't hit the massive creature running straight at her.

Marcus hit her at full speed, throwing her ten feet in the air and twenty feet backward. She landed in a heap and rolled down the bank. No one knew if she lived or died. The alpha stood overlooking Char, but only for an instant.

Long enough for Terry Henry Walton, expert Marine Corps marksman, to send a round behind the Werewolf's left shoulder. Marcus yipped like a wounded pup. Clyde picked up on the creature's pain and started to bray. He crouched as if he was going to run, but Terry yelled.

The alpha jumped down the bank and powered straight toward Char. She dodged, as she'd been practicing, avoiding his jaws and sinking her teeth into his neck as he passed.

He was wider than she remembered, and he jammed her hard with his shoulder as he leapt skyward. She lost her grip and fell in his wake, rolling to get back on her feet.

Terry fired and instantly dropped the weapon as the alpha continued toward him, leaving Char on the ground. Terry couldn't uncoil the bullwhip quickly enough, so he pulled his knife with his left hand and waited to dodge the incoming freight train.

Marcus was in pain, but his anger was overwhelming. There she was, with the human. It drove him beyond the edge of reason. The small man's heart would be his and Char, he could tell, was in heat. Wolf pups. He would make them this very night while dancing in the blood of the dead.

Terry wondered how much silver it would take to affect the massive beast. He didn't think he had enough, no matter what.

He stabbed at the paw that came for his head, leaving a clean slice on the outside of the Werewolf's leg. Marcus kicked hard with his back legs, catching Terry Henry in the mid-section.

Terry went down as if a pile driver hit him. He gasped as all the air was forced from him. His knife was gone. Marcus hit the ground, stopped on a dime and turned, his massive jaws heading straight for Terry's face.

Char's silver belly fur flew over Terry's face. She landed on Marcus's head with her front paws. She held his head down as she attempted to clamp her jaws on the black beast's neck. It was too wide and she only got a mouthful of hair and skin, but her fangs ripped inward.

Marcus stood on his back legs and roared his pain. Clyde darted in and bit the alpha's back leg, but the Werewolf kicked him away as if shaking off a fly. James and Devlin were ready to fire, but Char covered Marcus's back. They didn't have a clean shot.

Marcus dropped to all fours, vaulted over Terry, and ran straight for the bonfire with Char bouncing around on his back. He slid to a stop, ducked his head, and arched upward. Char flew from him and into the fire. She kicked through it and ran out the far side, hitting the ground and rolling to put out the flames.

Marcus stalked to the side, trapping Char between the fire and the riverbank.

Shots rang out. Dust puffed from Marcus's hide where the bullets impacted. James and Devlin kept firing. Char scrambled up the bank behind the bonfire, escaping the alpha's trap.

He turned and growled, his yellow eyes glowing as he raged. Blood ran from the gash on his leg. There had been very little silver on Terry's bullets and those wounds hurt, but they were starting to heal. The regular bullets just made him angry, and he'd had enough. He charged to his right and up the bank.

"Get down here!" Terry yelled as he tried to stand. His stomach hurt and he thought a couple ribs might be broken. Char was nowhere to be seen.

The two men jumped from the top of the bank and landed in the soft dirt, sliding down until they were at the bottom. The alpha leapt after them, creating a mini-avalanche when he hit the soft ground. He tried to push off, but the dirt gave way and he fell, sliding face first down the hill.

James and Devlin jumped to the side as the Werewolf slid in between them. James spun and snap fired into the vast black side. He pulled the trigger quickly, unable to flip the lever to automatic as he stumbled backwards. Marcus jumped toward him and Devlin fired into his back leg until the bolt locked to the rear. He fumbled for another magazine.

Marcus grabbed James in his great jaws, shook his head and threw the man aside. He turned and jumped, but his back leg failed him. He staggered forward and bit the rifle, yanking it from Devlin's hands.

Char howled her challenge from atop the riverbank. Her purple eyes glowed with her fury. They stood like two beacons, auroras calling to the alpha. He stood transfixed, giving his leg time to heal. He scrambled up the bank behind him, looking like he was running from Char's challenge.

She jumped down the bank, running to the bottom.

"No!" Terry yelled, expecting the alpha to leap back into the ravine to land on her.

He didn't. The fire snapped and popped. Clyde barked and pranced. A slight breeze blew across the Wastelands.

"Where is he, Char?" Terry asked as he struggled to stay upright.

She growled and snapped her jaws. Terry couldn't understand her when she was in Werewolf form. He splashed through the small stream and stood on the opposite side, not far from Char. He uncoiled his whip and waited.

James groaned in agony. Devlin crawled through the soft dirt at the bottom of the bank to get to him. There was nothing he could do to help James, but he took his rifle, crouching to remain between the corporal and the Werewolf.

Marcus howled from somewhere beyond the riverbank, not far away but not close. Char howled in reply, muscles tensed. She looked to be uninjured, despite getting thrown into a roaring bonfire.

Her eyes continued to radiate their purple glow. "That didn't go too badly," Terry said, laughing. It was the Marine's way to joke during a battle. It was too easy to get lost in the black and white world of combat's life and death. One wrong move and you could die. You could do everything right and still die. Sometimes the reaper cleaned house. When it was your time, it was your time.

No sense crying like a baby. A Marine's mettle was based on his ability to sow death and destruction, while at the same time having fun. Not too much fun, just enough that when the reaper knocked, you could laugh one last time.

Fuck that guy.

"My gut hurts," Terry said out loud.

Char growled and crouched.

"Go time, mother fucker!" Terry yelled into the darkness as he twirled the bullwhip beside him. Marcus arced high over the ravine as he jumped toward his mate. Her muscles uncoiled and she darted underneath him.

Terry snapped his wrist, aligned the whip with where Marcus was going to land, and watched the tip lash forward. The great black Werewolf was hit! The whip cracked and wrapped halfway around his neck. The silver of the necklace tore deep. Terry yanked the whip back, tearing skin and hide away from Marcus's throat.

Marcus reared back and howled his pain to the stars of the night sky. Terry took one step closer for a second try with his whip, but Marcus bolted away, jumping off a vertical bank to turn and face his enemies.

His dangerous enemies.

They all needed to die. *He was done playing.*

Devlin fired, hitting the Werewolf again and again. The bolt locked and he smoothly changed magazines.

Marcus was done getting used for target practice. He ran wide, like the wind, his back leg functional after giving it time to heal. He circled and lined up for his attack on Devlin.

The young man never knew what hit him as Marcus seized his upper body in his jaws and bit down, crushing Devlin's chest. The Werewolf tossed the body to the side, keeping his head low to protect his neck. Char started circling him, assuming the role of aggressor.

There's nothing more dangerous than a wounded animal that is cornered.

"Watch out, Char!" Terry called.

"Your human boy-toy wants you to be careful," Marcus growled at Char.

"At his worst, he's better than you've ever been," she replied, goading, egging him on.

"How often is he at his worst?" Marcus countered, watching her carefully. She was uninjured and he needed to heal. Whatever hellfire came from that whip was causing him enough anguish that he considered retreating and coming back another day.

Terry angled away from Char, trying to find an opening where he could use his whip again. Did he see Marcus wince?

The Werewolf backed up and turned, darting away, trying to keep Char between him and the whip.

"Got an ouchie?" Char taunted.

Marcus lunged. Char dodged, but not quickly enough as he powered into her, driving his back legs until they both rolled, snapping and biting. Char twisted wildly as she tried to get out from under the alpha.

He bit her side and pinned her to the ground.

Crack! The tip of the whip ripped across Marcus's rib cage, a second time lashed into his back leg. Marcus let go and jumped away, out of range of the whip.

Char stood, bleeding heavily from the deep bite. She staggered.

Marcus charged, ramming her with his shoulder and bowling her over as he headed straight for the human.

Terry snapped the whip back as Marcus's jaws drove straight for his chest. The tip of the bullwhip wrapped once more around the Werewolf's throat. Terry twisted until he thought his back would break. Marcus's jaws scraped across the front of his chest, tearing his shirt and slashing into the skin and muscle.

Terry caught the looped whip and pulled tightly as he was dragged alongside the massive beast. Marcus bucked and tried to shake his head, but the pain was too great. The whip found the gash of the previous injury and was digging through the muscle and into his throat.

The pain! The flame of the sun was pouring through the wound. He kicked with a front paw, trying to dislodge the human. Then he hit the ground and rolled, trapping Terry beneath him.

Terry couldn't breathe and his arms were pinned. He couldn't pull the whip tighter. He gasped and struggled.

For a moment, the weight became heavier. He tightened the muscles in his chest to keep the bones from cracking. His injured ribs screamed in agony.

Then Marcus was pulled from him as Char dragged the great black beast backward by the throat. The whip was pulled from his hand. With a last shake, Char ended Marcus's life.

Terry dragged himself to her. She couldn't lift her head, resting it between her paws on the ground. There was an ugly cut on the side of her face in addition to the bite in her side.

Terry's whip, she'd dug in and finished the alpha, even with the pain from Margie Rose's necklace digging into her.

"You're a warrior, Char," Terry said as he stroked her face.

She changed back into human form. The light from the bonfire showed that she had been injured far worse than what he could see before. Her skin bubbled in places from where she'd gone into the bonfire. Dark purple surrounded

183

missing flesh on her side. And the gash on the side of her face was raw and deep.

He pulled Char to him, cradling her as she moaned in agony.

"That could have gone better," he said, as was his way during combat.

"I think we did pretty well, don't you, Colonel?" Char gasped one word at a time.

"Indeed, Major. The battle is won, we just need to recover our wounded, bury our dead, and prepare for the next battle." Terry gently stroked her hair as she relaxed against him.

"That easy, huh?"

"I don't know how you keep ending up naked and in my arms. People are going to talk," Terry said.

"I really could give a fuck," Char replied, smiling as much as she could. "I need to rest and I need meat, as much as you can find."

Terry propped Char against the dead Werewolf and rushed to the fire to find her clothes, bringing them back in short order. There was no way she was going to get her jeans on in her current condition, so he removed his torn shirt and draped it over her.

"My Knight of the Round Table," she murmured.

"Try not to bleed on that. I just got it how I liked it," he said quietly, holding her face in his hand. She looked tired. Her eyes no longer glowed like purple fireflies.

"Of course you did," she snickered, wincing at the pain. "For the record, I feel like shit."

"That makes two of us," Terry agreed. Clyde whimpered as he appeared next to them. He walked stiffly, but wasn't bleeding and nothing looked broken. He laid down next to

Char, resting his head in her lap as she reclined into the dead alpha's fur.

Terry left them there and splashed two steps across the river as he headed for James and Devlin.

Terry knew as soon as he saw. Devlin was dead, his chest crushed by Marcus's jaws. Terry kneeled and closed the young man's eyes. He next went to James, who was injured but alert.

"I think I've got a broken leg and a rib or three," he said, grimacing as he talked.

"We'll get you fixed up. It's done. We did what we had to do and you stood your ground, like a real warrior. I'm proud to have you in the Force," Terry said softly, resting his hand lightly on the young man's shoulder.

"Gerry! Get down here," Terry yelled as he stood and went in search of Lacy.

Terry heard the horses splashing in the river as Geronimo approached. "What the fuck are you doing? We've got injured people down here and you bring the horses?"

"Oh shit! I'm sorry, Colonel. Let me take them back up stream, hobble them, and then I'll be back," Gerry apologized.

"Wait!" Terry called as he pulled the saddle bags from his horse, then he waved the young man away. Terry took the bags to Char, who looked like she'd already fallen asleep. He put the bag next to her and pulled their complete stock of beef jerky that Antioch and Claire had given them.

Char sniffed at it, then opened her eyes. She took the first piece and fed it to Clyde. She offered Terry the second piece and he stood, putting his hands on his hips.

"I have to find Lacy," he said abruptly and walked off. Char didn't hesitate as she wolfed down the remainder of the stash, sharing only one more small piece with the dog.

Terry quickly found the young woman, lying almost in the river, not far from the bonfire that was starting to burn down.

He rolled her unconscious form over. He found a growing bump on her head, but that was the only injury. He splashed water on her until she came to. Her eyes remained unfocused as she stared at the fire.

"Come on, James needs some company," Terry told her as he lifted her, draping an arm over his shoulder. He bent his knees to be closer to her level. She leaned into him and a new wave of pain coursed through his body. He wondered how badly he was injured, expecting the nanocytes would take care of it.

He'd lost one person that night, and he'd lament Devlin's loss later, when they were settled and he could be sure that he'd lose no more.

CHAPTER NINETEEN

When morning came, Terry and Char stretched, having mostly healed during the night.

"We have to make sure he's dead," Char whispered, pointing to the great black Werewolf.

"He looks plenty dead to me," Terry replied.

Char shook her head. "Cut off his head with your silver blade. There's no coming back from that." She tilted her head. "Well?"

"Are you the alpha now?" Terry asked, as he recovered his knife from where it had been thrown the night before. She tipped her head as if looking over the top of glasses, her purple eyes staring at him, unrelenting. "Fine."

It took ten minutes of hard work to finish the deed and he was up to his elbows in blood by the end of it. He kicked the head to the side and washed up in the river's trickle of water.

They then surveyed the damage.

Clyde was stiff but hungry, which they took as a good sign. James looked to be on death's doorstep. He was pasty white, and his breathing was shallow. At least his leg wasn't broken, Terry thought.

Lacy was out of it, her head lolling as she remained incapable of focusing. Gerry had done what he could during the night--cold compresses, plenty of water--but there wasn't anything else to do.

Terry closed his eyes and recalled the medical book he'd read. The symptoms suggested that James may have internal injuries.

"I think we might have to open him up," Terry suggested.

"What?" That surprised Char. "Don't tell me you're a doctor?"

"No, but I read this book once." When Terry heard himself say it, he realized how lame it sounded.

"Really? You read a book and now you're okay with cutting him open? And you plan to do it in the middle of the Wastelands?" Char was skeptical.

"He's not looking good and Lacy has a concussion. We're in a deep pile of shit. Things may fix themselves, but maybe they won't. We'll see what today brings and decide when we must." Terry looked concerned at James, who was sweating, cold, and clammy. He seemed delirious.

"Keep your eyes on them, Gerry. We have two graves to dig, and then we need to hunt, find something to eat, because I don't think we're leaving any time soon." Terry pursed his lips and looked around for something to dig with. They'd already scrounged the driftwood from places nearby.

Char offered to turn into a Werewolf and dig out a grave using her mad canine digging skills, but Terry declined since she refused to dig a grave for Marcus.

Terry grabbed a horse, saddled it, and rode up river until he found what he was looking for. He brought his piece of driftwood back to the camp and found Char digging with a flat round piece of rock. He looked at it and thought it would work better, but he was too stubborn to change. He removed his uniform shirt and attacked the dirt with newfound energy.

Char leaned back to watch.

"It goes faster if we both work at the same time," he suggested to her in between digs in the softer dirt of the riverbank.

"It might," she conceded, while kicking back, looking at him oddly.

"What?" Terry asked.

"Dig enough of a hole and then we can knock that hillside down on top of it. Not a shortcut, but a way to put them both into a more permanent place," Char offered.

Terry checked the area. The bank didn't look too sturdy. He nodded in agreement, then went back to digging. He tried to drag the decomposing, stinking Werewolf to the ditch that he'd dug, but even with his enhanced strength, Marcus was too heavy.

"Come on, Char. We're going to be here for a while. Do you really want that thing to be right in the middle of us all?" She reluctantly agreed and grabbed a paw, dragging the behemoth to the trench and rolling him in. Terry thought he'd dug it deeply enough, but that wasn't the case.

Devlin's grave looked small and insignificant next to that of the Werewolf. Terry, Char, and Geronimo stood together. They looked to Terry to say the words.

It was the colonel's duty.

"I hadn't known Devlin for long, but what he showed me was his spirit. He didn't take shit from people, and he was quick to lend a helping hand. Of the four tough guys I ran across my first day in town, he was the one I knew would sway the others to a better way. He brought Mark on board and the rest is history. Here we are, planting him in the ground, and that sucks. He deserved better, but for a Marine, for a member of the Force de Guerre, there is no higher honor than giving your life for your friend. James lives because Devlin put himself in between the enemy and an injured man. Devlin fought to the end, firing until his rifle was empty and he was no more. I salute you," Terry ended, snapping to attention and delivering a crisp salute.

Marine Corps style.

They used the flat rock and the driftwood to fill in some of the dirt, then Terry climbed to the top of the bank, found a weak spot, and dug in until it gave way. He jumped back just in time to keep from going with it. The dirt rolled over top of the two graves.

Terry slid down the bank and tamped the graves down. He positioned his piece of driftwood as a monument at Devlin's head. They left Marcus's grave unmarked.

James looked no worse and Lacy was still out of it.

"We need to find food," Terry said, looking at Char. "Do you sense anything close?"

She shook her head.

Terry turned to Geronimo. "We're going to ride out, find something, and then we'll be back. There's nothing left out there, so the next thing you'll hear will be us. Don't be afraid."

"Why would I be afraid? I have my friends the horses nearby. They'll watch out for me and I'll watch out for these two. The sooner you go, the sooner you'll get back. We're all hungry," Gerry said, encouraging the major and the colonel to get on the road.

❖ ❖ ❖

Even traveling along the river, the conditions were harsh. Antioch and his family only managed ten miles the first day and fifteen the second. On the third day, they struggled to go just five miles. At least the mountains were rising in the distance. The goal was in sight, although still a long way off.

The children were bored and the cattle started to meander, requiring more breaks in the river. There was plenty to drink, but little to eat. The cows tried to graze what little growth was available along the riverbanks, while Antioch, Claire, and the children made do with what they had--a total of five days' worth of beef jerky.

Antioch declared half-rations at the end of day three, hoping that it would carry them through to the foothills, where it would be cooler and they could make up ground. As long as they had water, they'd survive, but that wasn't enough. They were surviving where they'd been.

This was an idiot's quest and they'd come too far to turn back.

"I think we may have made a mistake," Antioch said to his wife.

"Not at all, Antie. We will put our faith in the Lord and continue to His promised land. If we don't, we leave our boys to lives of loneliness and they will be the last generation of the Weathers family. I don't want that. Besides, I don't know if I'll ever be able to wash the dirt of the Wastelands from my body, but I can try in the new place," Claire said with a smile.

It wasn't an act. She was genuinely happy with life and

kept the family going in the right direction.

"I don't know why I doubted. God bless you, Claire Weathers," the old man said, continuing to amble ahead, leaning heavily on his walking stick, which was also useful for swatting kids and cows alike.

❖ ❖ ❖

Terry, Char, and Clyde rode out quickly, heading east, downriver. Terry counted on Char's ability to sense game to guide them, but she wasn't feeling anything.

Clyde was perched in Terry's lap. "Are you the alpha now?" Terry asked.

"Maybe. Usually it's the largest male, but times change, don't they?" Char answered, looking for signs of game, sniffing the air, watching for movement. "The pack would have to accept me as the alpha, but they'd fall in line quickly after the initial rough and tumble."

"Are you returning to the pack?" Terry asked, focusing on Char's face. The scar from silver necklace stood out, twisting the corner of one lip. It looked like it had healed as much as it was going to heal. He didn't think it detracted from her beauty, but added to it because he knew how she got it, the risk she took.

She caught him staring. "Why, TH, who would have thought you'd get all shmoopy over a little ol' Werewolf."

"I'm not shmoopy. What the hell does that even mean anyway? That's some serious fucking bullshit right there! You can't just make up words and then hang them around my neck like some anvil!" Terry retorted, ending with a snort.

"Anvil?" she accused, giving Terry the stink eye.

"That's not what I meant," he grumbled. "What's in a

name? That which we call a rose by any other name would smell as sweet. *Romeo and Juliet*, Act II, Scene II."

"The lady doth protest too much, methinks. *Hamlet*, Act III, Scene II," Char replied.

"Do you think I am easier to be played on than a pipe? Same act and scene," Terry countered.

"Can one desire too much of a good thing? *As You Like It*, Act IV, Scene I." Char rode close, pulling back on the reins to stop Terry's horse. They sat side by side.

"All the world 's a stage, and all the men and women merely players. They have their exits and their entrances; And one man in his time plays many parts. *As You Like It*, Act II, Scene VII," Terry whispered.

Char's eyes lit up like purple sparklers. "Say it," she insisted.

"What?"

"Just say it, tough guy." She smiled, her scar tugging her lip down on one side of her face.

"You know," he replied, unable to take his eyes from the Werewolf.

She looked away quickly and sniffed the air. "Saved by a pig, how appropriate, don't you think, TH?"

"I like this place and willingly could waste my time in it. *As You Like It*, Act II, Scene IV," Terry said as Char spurred her mount, riding toward the sound and the smell of a javelina.

CHAPTER TWENTY

After they'd eaten a couple times, James looked respectable, the color having returned to his face. Char was pleased that Terry wasn't going to perform exploratory surgery on the young man.

Lacy was still out of it. The lump on her head was the size of a golf ball. They kept it wet, so the evaporating water could keep it cool, but that wasn't the biggest problem. A concussion could take days or even weeks to heal. The jarring ride on a horse wouldn't be best, but it was the only way they had to get back. They couldn't stay where they were. They'd keep running out of food until they couldn't find any more.

They loaded the horses and began walking. Five people and eight horses headed west, staying close to the river to take frequent breaks, but they still spent a long time in the saddle. Lacy almost fell off twice, so Gerry rode with her to hold her in place.

They had used some of Devlin's clothes as bandages and bundled James's ribs tightly. James gritted his teeth. The act of riding, even at a walk, was painful.

They ran out of food at the end of the second day. They went without on the third day. No one talked as the horses ambled ahead, having eaten little themselves. There was plenty of water and they knew they'd survive, but misery kept their stomachs company.

On the fourth day, they caught up to Antioch, Claire, and their family. The cows had decided that they weren't going to walk any further and the poor people didn't have the energy to encourage them.

The worst part was that the town ahead was only a couple miles away. Within, there was a lake and grass. Terry and Char gave up their horses and they mounted the Weathers family, all fourteen of them, on five horses and told them to ride ahead.

"Geronimo, you're in charge since you know where you're going. Take these people to the lake, we'll be along shortly with the cattle," Terry ordered.

"Yes, sir!" the young man replied. "Colonel? What happens if you don't show up?"

"Then ride back out here and get us. The cows leave an unmistakable trail." Terry slapped the horse's rump and watched as Geronimo led the horses toward the ruins of the town ahead.

Terry, Char, and Clyde climbed down the riverbank and helped themselves to a drink of water.

"So, we're just going to run around and slap cow butts to get them to move?" Char asked, knowing that wasn't what Terry had in mind.

"I thought we could encourage them in a slightly

different way," Terry said, casually running one finger down the buttons of her shirt.

"Really? We're going to make love and that will get the cows running?"

Terry leaned back. "No. I was thinking a little Werewolf action, stampede them right up the river," he said, happy with himself.

"Listen, I don't Werewolf at your beck and call. Who is whose pet here?" Char asked.

"No one is anyone's pet!" Terry crossed his arms and stood tall. Char smirked at him.

"Colonel."

"Major."

"Do you really think of me as a sheep dog?" Char asked, hands on her hips, defiant. "I get it! I'm just an asset. Well, Terry Henry Walton, you can kiss this asset goodbye. Get the cows yourself!"

Char turned and stormed off.

"Get the fuck back here! What the hell do you think you're doing? These cattle are life and fucking death for a whole community!"

Char kept walking. Terry ran past her, then turned and blocked her way.

"Let me by," she demanded.

He stood there, mouth set and arms crossed.

Not the best stance to start a fight, as he found out. Char casually took one step forward, then swung an uppercut that caught him below his crossed arms, lifting him off the ground and throwing him backwards.

She dove after him, but he'd gotten his legs up and she landed on his feet. Terry threw her over his head. He rolled and stood, ready in his fighting stance.

Char's eyes glowed purple with her fury. She charged and he dodged to punch as she passed, but it was a feint. She sidestepped with him at the last moment and he found himself face to face with someone who was stronger and faster.

She lashed out repeatedly toward his head and he blocked most, but too many punches still got through. He tried to put more space between them, but Char was relentless.

He dropped straight down, throwing his head one way and twisting, sweeping a leg through her knees. Char buckled and fell backwards. Terry ran five steps ahead and turned, crouching.

"Would you fucking stop!?" Terry yelled. She approached in a combat stance. Terry's adrenaline was surging. "I have no idea what the fuck I did to set you off, but if this is what you want, so be it."

She angled in, but he wouldn't let himself get pinned. She came straight, ducked left, dodged right, went low with a sweep of her own. Terry jumped it, but when he came down, she was already standing and swinging.

He blocked the first punch, but the second to his groin doubled him over, gasping and gagging. She wrapped an arm around his throat, then pulled and rolled. He flew over top of her and slammed into the ground. Char straddled him, as she reached for his throat, but he caught her wrists.

Char ducked down to bite his fingers. Terry pulled her hands closer and head-butted the bridge of her nose. Stunned for an instant, Terry took advantage and rolled, pinning her beneath him.

He kept his knees spread to maintain leverage as he held her wrists.

"Calm the fuck down!" he begged her. Char's eyes stopped glowing and started sparkling anew. "What did I do?"

"You assumed," she replied in a calm voice. Blood ran from her nose and down her cheeks. It filled her new scar before continuing to her neck.

Terry rocked back to his feet and stood, pulling Char upright with him.

"What?" he asked, confused.

"Why didn't you just ask me? Of course I'll Werewolf for you, if you only ask and are ready for me to say no, just in case. But you assumed, made all the decisions, didn't you, Colonel?" Char raised her eyebrows to make her point.

"But it was the logical thing to do. I thought you would have already figured it out," Terry countered weakly.

"Listen here, Mister Terry Henry Walton, don't try that 'don't be stupid' routine on me. We think of different things in different ways, so never assume anything. If you have any intention of courting me, it's as an equal partner, do you get me?" She angled her head, mouth set, and glared at him.

"Court you?" Terry asked, earning him a punch in the chest.

Char grabbed his collar and pulled his face down to hers. He didn't resist. She brushed her lips over his, across his cheek, and to his ear. "You need to stop fucking around, TH. You are missing out on an awful lot of what makes life worth living," she whispered.

Terry pinched his eyes shut. A wife, a child, both dead. His heart torn apart. His soul blackened. The nanocytes kept him alive so he could relive his failure to protect them, over and over. When Margie Rose's one kind act freed him from his abyss, he committed to bring civilization back to humanity.

He didn't deserve anything for himself. At least that was what he'd been telling himself. He opened the door just a crack and peeked in to see if there was any room left in civilization for him, enough humanity for Terry to experience some for himself.

"Is this how it works in Werewolf land? If you like someone, you beat the holy crap out of them?" he finally asked, running one hand over his battered face and caressing Char's neck with the other.

She chuckled. "Kind of, but not really. You made me mad."

"And you punched me in the balls," he answered. "Even?"

Terry stepped back and offered to shake hands, secure the truce, but Char pulled him back to her. She closed her eyes, one hand on his cheek. He leaned down, wrapping his arms around her as their lips met.

The fire. The surge in emotions. The pain.

"Ow!" he exclaimed. "My lips hurt."

"Mine, too, you big bully. How dare you punch me in the face!"

Char stripped, trying to make a show for Terry, but she was too stiff and sore. Terry didn't think he'd had an effect during the fight, but her body was covered in bruises. He almost felt bad, but remembered his own pain and how the nanocytes were working overtime to repair the damage.

She changed into a sleek brown Werewolf, then nuzzled him and he scratched behind her ears, caressed her sides. Clyde started barking from the riverbank.

For the first time ever, Char dropped into play pose, challenging Clyde, who started barking up a storm. She raced up the bank after him and the two ran into the waste, frolicking.

"May you live in interesting times," he told himself.

EPILOGUE

Billy watched a menagerie of people and cows strolling up the road. He turned his head back toward the house. "Felicity!" he yelled. "You might want to come out here."

Felicity appeared, pulling her jacket tightly around her. Billy wrapped a protective arm around her as the group approached. Terry and Char were in the middle, leading horses that carried three people each.

They heard someone yelling and whistling in the back of the group to keep the cows soldiering on. Billy and Felicity took positions astride the flower beds to keep them from getting trampled, although the horses made their way unerringly to them with each visit.

Clyde ran ahead to greet Billy and Felicity, getting his head petted by each, before getting pushed away when he tried to stuff his nose between Felicity's legs. She kicked at him as he ran off. The rabbit population required his attention.

"We brought some company," Terry offered with a smile, and then introduced Antioch and Claire, who chased the kids from the horses as they dismounted. They lined up the twelve youngsters, who looked warily at the men carrying rifles.

Mark saluted and Terry returned it. "Stand down and disband the guard!" Terry ordered.

Billy clapped his hands and then slapped Terry on the shoulder. He turned to Char and stopped. "What happened to you?"

"Marcus was a little harder to put down than your average rabid dog," she replied coldly.

"I see," Billy said, examining the scar. "A shame."

Char held her head up, proudly, radiantly. Terry couldn't help but smile.

"Billy, the only thing changed is we are safer than we were. That's what matters. What do you say we put up the Weathers family by the road south. There are two fields to put the cattle into. Fatten them up and encourage them to procreate. You have to know something about animal husbandry, don't you, Billy?" Terry jibed.

"I am sure that I should be offended, but you are such a hunk of man candy, Terry Henry Walton, that I can find no anger to throw your way," Felicity drawled. Terry beamed his best smile. Even though his face still hurt from the pounding Char had given him, the bruises were gone.

Terry turned serious and looked at Billy. "We lost Devlin, and Lacy took a shot to the head. She's got a concussion. James has some broken ribs, but is on the mend. Everyone did well. They stood tall before the enemy," Terry reported.

"He was a big fucker," Billy said sympathetically.

"Yeah, something like that, but we found really good people out there. Antioch, Claire, and their kids are going to help us grow," Terry suggested, sweeping an arm to take in the big family. The old couple nodded and smiled. "We could use some food. It was a rough trip out of the Wastelands for them."

Billy sent Mark and Boris to load up from one of the freezers. Antioch sent his older children to help.

When they returned, it was time for everyone to go their own way.

"Mark, take the members of the Force to the barracks and get them and the horses settled. The major and I will show this good people their new home and fields, and then we'll find you first thing tomorrow and get back on track with the training."

"Where are you going to take us next, TH?" Billy asked. Terry bristled as he did not yet consider Billy a friend, although the smaller man was growing on him.

He paused, then decided to let it go.

"I have some ideas," Terry said, leaving everything unsaid. "We'll be by sometime tomorrow."

Terry turned before Billy could reply. He and Char helped Claire and Antioch onto the horses. The group slowly moved on, horses, people, and cows heading toward a new life.

❖ ❖ ❖

"We don't have what we need, no matter how much you yell and stamp your feet!" Merrit told Timmons for the third time.

"I want to blow shit up!" he howled.

"We both do, but we need to go at this a little different way. How about a nitrate bomb? We can build us a cart to haul the damn thing and then, kaboom!" Merrit suggested, smiling.

They sat within an old lab of the Air Force Academy. Debris from the ruined building had blocked the entrance. They'd spent days clearing it before finally gaining access. The lab was mostly intact because it had been inaccessible, but the chemicals were in a poor state. They hadn't kept well for twenty years.

The petroleum-based liquids, those things that Timmons wanted most, had either evaporated, gotten contaminated with moisture, or the container had failed. Some other chemicals were surprisingly intact, having been stored better or maybe just luckier.

"Can we make gunpowder?" Timmons asked.

"We can always make gunpowder, but we need to dig up a few other chemicals that we should be able to find in the hills. Electricity would be nice to help us grind the ingredients," Merrit suggested.

"Then that's what we need to do," Timmons said, far more calmly. Even if it took a month, at least they would be working toward something more than just eating and existing. There was plenty for every member of the pack to do. Saltpeter, sulfur, and charcoal, all ground to a fine powder.

Timmons didn't know why he had fixated on TATP or TNT, when something like gunpowder was significantly easier to produce and would fill the gap until they had something more powerful.

If anyone tried to challenge his leadership, he'd be ready. If Marcus returned, he'd be ready for him, too. They were going to build a new world, where Werewolves were at the center.

No one could stand up to them. The Forsaken, TQB, and all the rest. They hadn't heard from them in decades. They were all gone, just like everyone else. Timmons's lip curled as he snarled at those who had gone before, those who had hung him and his pack out to dry. He accepted the challenge to rectify that.

"Time to get to work," Timmons told his fellow Were-wolf.

THE END

OF

NOMAD REDEEMED

Terry Henry Walton will return
in Nomad Unleashed, February 2017

AUTHOR'S NOTES - CRAIG MARTELLE

Written: January 9, 2017

I'm a lifelong daydreamer and student of human interaction. I have some degrees, but those don't matter when it comes to telling the story. Engaging characters within a believable narrative- that's what it's all about. I live in the interior of Alaska, far away from an awful lot, but I love it here. It is natural beauty at its finest.

We love Alaska, but sometimes you just have to get away. We spent a week in Hawai'i while the final edits were taking place on Nomad Redeemed in early January, 2017. Alaska is so cold and dark, it takes going somewhere light and warm to recharge the bodies and power through the rest of winter.

So we did, but that didn't hold us back from reaching out and working to make Nomad Redeemed a worthy successor to Nomad Found. Plus, I was able to start Nomad Unleashed while on the plane here. I had to flesh out a few ideas and get the story off right with a little action, a little insight into where Terry is taking the Force de Guerre.

Yes, my style is a little different from Michael's and this story arc starts in a post-apocalyptic world, but eventually, the FDG will make it into space as a group that Bethany Anne can send to the universe's hot spots that don't rise to the attention of the Queen's Bitches.

In the interim, Terry needs to help bring the world back to a civilized state. Much work to do and only a limited amount of time – only 130 years!

Thank you to those who've read Nomad Found and left reviews! You warm my heart, and I listen to your comments. We'll continue to improve the three-dimensional view of the characters as you've asked while keeping the action going. It is a dynamic world in which TH and Char live.

Diane Velasquez and Dorene Johnson are perpetually ready to lend a helping hand by reading a passage and telling me how it resonates. Kat Lind has been a force of nature in making me a better writer because she makes me want to be a better writer. Some of my newest readers are making this a fun trip, along with some stalwart folks who joined me in the Free Trader series – Sherry Foster, Melissa Ratcliffe, Norman Meredith, Nipa Jhaveri, Heath Felps, and so many more. If I left you off, it was unintentional and everyone deserves a mention.

The editor and publisher of my post-apocalyptic End Times Alaska series is also on board and working to make sure that the final book of that series comes out at the same time as Nomad Redeemed. Thank you! Monique Lewis Happy for keeping my books relevant in both the traditionally published and self-published world. A rising tide floats all boats, as I like to say.

And one final thank you to Michael Anderle for driving this train. The Kurtherian Gambit is a great series with an endless universe of stories. I appreciate the opportunity to fill in one small gap of time in one tiny place on the third rock from the sun.

Peace to all – time to get back to work on Nomad Unleashed. TH & Char have city-states to dismantle and rebuild. So much work to do, but with the power of a bullwhip and keen minds, they have a plan…

❖ ❖ ❖

If you liked this story, you might like some of my other books.

You can join my mailing list by dropping by my website www.craigmartelle.com or if you have any comments, shoot me a note at craig@craigmartelle.com. I am always happy to hear from people who've read my work. I try to answer every email I receive.

If you liked the story, please write a short review for me on Amazon. I greatly appreciate any kind words, even one or two sentences go a long way. The number of reviews an ebook receives greatly improves how well an ebook does on Amazon.

Amazon – www.amazon.com/author/craigmartelle
Facebook – www.facebook.com/authorcraigmartelle
My web page – www.craigmartelle.com
Twitter – www.twitter.com/rick_banik

Thank you for reading Nomad Redeemed!

AUTHOR'S NOTES - MICHAEL ANDERLE

Written: January 14, 2017

As always, can I say with a HUGE amount of appreciation how much it means to me that you not only read this book, but you are reading these notes as well?

(Quick note, Please read the end comments related to Craig's Trad Pubbed book later.)

So, how can everything go right, and wrong, in the space of 48 hours? (Warning - RANT coming ahead!)

On the wrong side - please don't ever ask a romance writer if a Romance book (notice the capital 'R') needs an HEA? (Happy Ever After - or HEA for Now). Now, this story is coming from the 20Books group (Indie Authors supporting each other), and the individual who asked the question just wanted to know the answer. You know, a simple *yes* or *no*?

Unfortunately, there were those who decided they wanted to *argue* the point.

Now, I happened to be editing Claimed By Honor (with Justin Sloan) on this particular day, and only kinda knew what was going on when someone had decided to jump out of the group due to 'stuff said' and personally messaged me they were leaving.

I'm not into angst, anger, harsh words…It just isn't me at all. (Mind you, I FEEL these emotions a fair amount of times, but I don't like being a part of arguments because… arguments!) Further, when I saw another post by a person I admire the next morning, who was still feeling emotions over this discussion in the 20Books group, it sucked for me to know it sucked for her.

In the end, I would have personally told those arguing the facts. The fact that Romance (the category) has a MAJOR trope called the HEA. If you choose not to abide by the trope and then label your book a Romance, you are going to go down in a flaming mess. That a person doesn't like the idea the category 'Romance' needs an HEA doesn't change the reality of readers expectations.

Obviously, this isn't true for 100% of all readers, but it is the vast majority. More than enough to kill the reviews for any particular book.

Once I told them this, I would tell them to go out and do what they are going to do based on the information. If they ignore the warning and should they get blasted to smithereens by reviews, don't say they weren't warned, or that the world was against them.

The World isn't anymore against them than if they jumped off a building and went SPLAT on the ground twenty stories below.

Gravity isn't against them, it just *is*.

(Speculation on Dark Matter / Dark Energy and entangled particles connected to gravity can be found here … What? You didn't think I dreamt up all this science stuff, right? (grin!) https://www.wired.com/2017/01/case-dark-matter/)

So, we had a ton of ignorance and a non-bliss discussion with (I think) over 300 replies. (I never did read the whole post, because of arguments, remember?) That was the sucky part of the last 48 hours since Claimed By Honor released.

On the positive side: family is good, Claimed By Honor went to at least #180 in the store, a best seller in multiple categories and Justin Sloan is a top 30 Science Fiction author again!

Oh, and yours truly is a top 100 author in all of Amazon for the fifth straight day.

<START RANT>

Because of my success, there is HUGE gnashing of teeth out in a couple of authoring groups about that damned Michael Anderle and his *fans*. (Apparently, you are now lumped in WITH me for being too stupid to understand what makes a good book - I'm assuming a good book is anything they write, I can't say, I haven't read them. I'm a pulp fiction writer; I write what I like to read and it so happens that a few others like these stories I write, too.)

Well, for those of you who have read these author notes from way back in the very beginning of The Kurtherian Gambit, you won't be surprised by my next sentence.

I've got my middle finger up to those who are still hating on us.

The haters can kiss my ever-loving-Indie-Publishing-Outlaw-Ass… My fans are the FUCKING BEST IN THE WORLD. (Ooops, there I went again, sticking 'yet another F*Bomb' in my book.) We are smart, intelligent, giving, supportive, and frankly, don't give a shit about their opinions. So, I WISH THEM THE BEST THAT LIFE HAS TO OFFER and a few suggestions, not the least of which is …

You be you, and let us be us.

We all have problems, and no life is perfect. But, my fans wouldn't enjoy my stories if they didn't appreciate justice, desire to see injustice served and enjoy the friendship and all around fun that the characters exhibit. Does this mean my fans DON'T like other types of books?

NO!

Many of you, my fans, read a ton of different genre's, support multiple authors, encourage people in remarkable ways and are amazing in your diversity… These grumbling individuals need to be careful they don't have an online fan riot backlash.

Because, if this stuff keeps up (attacking my fans). I'll track down their online internet conversations and personally and privately warn them they can say whatever they want about me… It comes with the territory of success.

But if they keep up with this speaking and slurring my fans?

Yeah, I'll shine a little light their way for doing that, and I don't think they will enjoy the discussions with so many pissed off, highly literate and well-read individuals.

<END RANT>

Now, here is the second of the Terry Henry Walton Chronicles, and I have to say I love this series! Yeah, it's different, but I damned well enjoy TH and Char and the rest. I hated that some of those friends from book 01 died, but gosh damn that dude was a colossal son-of-a-bitch!

What's going on with the rest of the pack? Is TH going to get GOOD beer (because, priorities, you know?) and will the mayor get the car running and I wonder whether Felicity will stay the ugly person she seems like she is, or will she change, too? This feels like a fun soap-opera to me, and I'm digging every damned page.

So, I'm grabbing the popcorn like so many others and popping it in my mouth, wondering what is coming up next?

Best Regards,
Michael Anderle

P.S. - Check out the first few chapters of End Times Alaska. It isn't in Kindle Unlimited (because it was

published by a traditional publisher who has constraints, I think). Who knows, maybe at some point in the future we can look to the merging of Indie and Trad Publishing as being supported by this book, right here. If the traditional publisher notices a lift in sales? We might change the future of how we (Trad Pub, Indie Author and Fans) all work together.

<NO! I am absolutely not swinging my Bethany Anne labeled Coca-Cola bottle and singing out loud in my kitchen, "I'd like to Teach the World to sing...">

(Actually, yes, yes I am.)

End Times Alaska - a four-book series about survival and life after the destruction of society in the frigid cold of interior Alaska.

"This book drew me in right away. I loved the characters and the descriptions of the area. I could almost see the place. It was really intense at some points. I loved the amount of detail used to describe how the people handled the sudden changes to their lifestyle. I was completely unable to put this book down," an Amazon five-star review.

Please enjoy the first two short chapters of ENDURE, book 01 in the series.

http://www.winlockpress.com

Why?

Smoke didn't billow from the barrel after I fired at the injured animal. I could see clearly the hole I'd blown through its chest. It had only been three days since the dog's humans had been home, but that was long enough.

The pair of dogs had fought viciously. One was dead and the other mortally wounded. I only put him out of his misery, at least that's what I told myself.

I'd broken through a window of a neighbor's home when I heard the pitiful wailing of the injured dog. I knew something was wrong when I heard it. A dog. Dying.

I couldn't leave it in pain, but that didn't make me feel any better.

It'd be best if I buried the two dogs, but temperatures were way too cold. What was it? Minus twenty Fahrenheit? Even the snow was frozen hard.

I left the dog where it lay, not far from its former house mate. I'd come back when it was warmer, before they started to decompose, and give them a proper burial.

I wondered how many times I'd tell myself that same story. I shoved the pistol, already cool after the shot, back into my pocket and put my glove on. I had the short walk home to think about how our lives had been a mere three days ago.

The Instant

It was Tuesday morning. My wife, Madison, was a professor and started later in the day, so she was still home. Students in college couldn't be bothered to get out of bed early. Life began at the crack of noon. This was the best for us as it fit our lifestyle. I'd retired from the Marines quite a few years back, and filled the role of house husband, kept man, whatever you wanted to call it. I was too busy with the kids to work. In a previous life, I was gone from home two weeks out of every month.

It all happened in an instant. There was a bright flash from over the hills. The power went out. A massive thunderclap followed. The windows shook, but only one pane shattered. A strange sensation passed through the sky, like a heat wave one would see around the flames of a bonfire. Then calm returned. But not the power.

"What the hell was that?" I asked. It was a rhetorical question, the kind people ask when they are afraid. Neither my wife nor our dog attempted to answer.

Our two-year-old twins stopped playing, and both began to cry.

We looked toward the city, the direction of the flash, although there were ten miles, two hills, and a stand of trees between us and Fairbanks. It was late morning, but still mostly dark. This far north, Alaska in the winter was a different world. The sun both rises and sets in the south. It stays mostly on the horizon, visible for less than four hours on the solstice.

We expected to see the house next door burning. The explosion seemed that close.

But it wasn't. Nothing shone in the darkness nearby. Through the trees and above the hills, we could see the moonlight reflecting off a growing mushroom cloud.

"I think something blew up. The base? Maybe the power plant?" I didn't know what else to say. I was thinking out loud, and it didn't make sense, not even to me. Something had just happened, and it wasn't good.

"Do you think the power will come back on?" my wife asked.

"Not anytime soon. I'll set up the generator." It was the usual twenty-below-zero Fahrenheit outside. Snow covered everything. The trees sparkled with the cold frost, even in the near dark. It was pleasant. A few cars were on Chena Hot Springs Road. I wasn't sure where they'd be going. No one could have missed the explosion. Then again, there were always the curious and the obtuse.

Our cell phones showed no service. Our back-up battery power strips didn't even beep. A power surge must have preceded the outage. The surge protectors appeared to be dead.

I dug out our wind-up radio and gave it to Madison. She could spin it to life and see what the news said. "Why don't we just use your battery-powered radio?" she suggested. It had been ten minutes since we lost power and I already acted like we had nothing left.

We had everything left. I got the other radio for her.

Nothing. Static on static. This was an all-purpose radio, so it also had sideband. There wasn't anything anywhere. Nothing but noise. She set it aside. It was more important to take care of the twins. Two-year-olds require a great deal of attention, no matter what else is going on. No matter what other so-called priorities may exist.

And our dog Phyllis needed to go outside.

I bundled us both up, and we went outside. She did her thing while I set up the generator...

Interested in Reading More?

Endure
https://www.amazon.com/dp/B01GQLVHXK

Run
https://www.amazon.com/dp/B01I45F494

Return
https://www.amazon.com/dp/B01JK7CHR2

Fury
https://www.amazon.com/dp/B01N0ZJMUJ

PLEASE NOTE!

These books are traditionally published and as such, aren't in Kindle Unlimited.

HOWEVER, they are available for purchase on Amazon as well as other platforms.

59600845R00130

Made in the USA
Middletown, DE
12 August 2019